The Boy with Six Fingers

A Novella

by

Barry Vitcov

Finishing Line Press
Georgetown, Kentucky

The Boy with Six Fingers

A Novella

Publisher: Leah Huete de Maines
Editor: Christen Kincaid
Cover Art: Jennifer Rood
Author Photo: William E. Saltzstein
Cover Design: Elizabeth Maines McCleavy

Order online: www.finishinglinepress.com
also available on amazon.com

Author inquiries and mail orders:
Finishing Line Press
PO Box 1626
Georgetown, Kentucky 40324
USA

Contents

Dedicated
to all who celebrate the uniqueness in ourselves
and the wisdom of elders,
and to those who took the time to read my manuscript and provide feedback:
Audrey, Charlie, Ken, Neal, Paula, Tia.

1

Seymour

Beige. The waiting room was beige with brown and cream highlights. The doctors who shared the space must have met and decided the most calming color, the drabness of beige, could anesthetize even the most anxious patient. Or maybe they attended a color theory workshop at a medical conference where they were exposed to theories suggesting certain colors were best in certain environments. Was pink the best calming color in jail cells? Light green in classrooms and prisons? Beige in waiting rooms?

The one exception to this mind-numbing interior landscape was found at the reception desk, where a young woman sat wearing an ugly Christmas sweater and red-ornament earrings. She didn't smile when I approached, probably because she had been trained to be serious with a neutral affect but did manage to welcome me by asking my name and birthdate. "Seymour, May 19, 1937, but call me Sy." She was not the usual front office receptionist and I noticed her name tag said, "Katie," a perky name for no doubt a perky young woman.

"Thank you. And your last name?" she asked.

"Seymour," I responded.

"Your last name, sir," she repeated.

"It's Seymour. Once you get to know me, you'll know my name is Seymour S. Seymour. My parents had a sense of humor. But, please, call me Sy. And don't bother asking what the S stands for, as if it isn't obvious enough."

Katie sat open mouthed for a moment before handing me a clipboard with several forms attached. I was fairly certain she wanted to laugh or maybe even smile but managed to maintain her blasé self. "We'll need to update your information. Please, have a seat and Dr. Chan will see you soon."

"Nothing has changed since I was here last time."

"I understand, but our system is always changing," said Katie following the script she had been trained to use. Lately, I had been noticing more and more how those in the helping professions are uniformly instructed in polite interactions. Receptionists, customer care representatives, even fast-food workers frequently begin interactions with "I understand, but." Someone somewhere is writing a standardized book of appropriate protocol for frontline workers. I wondered if simple courtesies were taught in families anymore. "Understanding" followed by a "but" seemed insincere.

I took the clipboard and sat on one of the straight-backed, slightly padded chairs and realized that all the other seats were empty. What did this mean? Was I the only one requiring medical attention? My need was not pressing. It was my semi-annual dermatological appointment and I would most likely have something frozen or cut off as a consequence of too much teenage sun. I had become well acquainted with the excision of pre-cancerous or basal cell growths at the hands of more than a dozen different dermatologists. I had outlived at least four who ironically died from melanomas and another half dozen who retired or found other more interesting professions. I really admired the one who decided to become a fishing guide and spend her days living in a small cabin in the woods with her five dogs and two cats. My current doctor was a recent graduate of Stanford Medical School who seemed much too enthusiastic when examining my imperfect body and flawed skin. He was sure to explain every anomaly he discovered with language I did not understand before I gave my approval to remove whatever problematic growth he found. I did enjoy how he ended each appointment by opening his smartphone to show me the latest family photos of his attractive wife and two preschool-aged sons. Much of the time, they were all wearing large floppy hats, which I suppose were protection from harmful solar exposure.

I continued to wait in the empty waiting room. I glanced over at Katie who was fixated on her computer monitor and clicking away at her keyboard. Maybe she was reading my information to confirm my identity. It wouldn't be the first time.

After Dr. Chan's examination, the freezing of just one skin anomaly, and the proud showing of recent family pictures, I walked home. I had recently moved into a nearby retirement complex after selling the home I had grown up in; the home I inherited from my parents who had inherited it from their parents. I lived with my wife until she died after almost fifty years of marriage and raised our three sons. It was a pleasant home with a tidy yard, aging roof, ancient heater, and in need of immediate plumbing and electrical upgrades. The young couple who purchased it had written a four-page letter detailing their love for a quaint, cottage-style home in need of the love and attention they would provide. After six months of love and attention they flipped it for an exorbitant profit.

I rehomed myself at the Visions of Eden Home for Active Seniors. My sons, daughters-in-law, and grandchildren all thought it was the right thing to do. They encouraged me to take advantage of all the social and extra-curricular activities offered; I have never been interested in being social and the water yoga, bridge, bocce ball, or the multitude of book clubs did not appeal to me. What I liked to do was take walks, aimless without-any-purpose walks. Visions of Eden was located off a boulevard lined by strip malls, apartment complexes, medical facilities, and every franchised fast and slow-food restaurant imagined by overly indulgent Americans. I include myself as one of those indulgent citizens who manage to stay thin despite my love for burgers, fries, shakes, tacos, chalupas, and ice cream sundaes. I believe it's the walking and constant water sipping that keeps me going. I briskly stride along, my Army surplus canteen attached to my olive-green utility belt while wearing light or heavyweight sweats depending on the season, enjoying the sights and sounds of commerce. I'm attracted to drive-thru lanes where consumers lean out their windows to order meals from disembodied voices. Lately, even if I don't have an appointment, I've been taking regular walks to my doctors' offices, usually Dr. Chan's, where I like to sit in the waiting room and observe.

Katie didn't notice me the first two times I entered without an appointment and took a seat on the beige chair in the far corner of the waiting room. Perhaps it was because the room was crowded. Or maybe it was because she was glued to her computer screen. Looking up and acknowledging people when they entered a bland room was apparently not in the receptionist training manual. Fortunately, Katie's affinity for colorful sweaters and earrings was enough to break the room's monotony. It was the third time when the room was empty and I initiated contact by saying, "Hi, Katie. How's your day going?"

She looked up and surprised me by responding, "Mr. Seymour, I don't believe you have an appointment."

"No. Not today. Just taking a walk. And, please, call me Sy."

She surprised me again by asking, "Weren't you just here the other day?"

"Yes, this is a good stop when I'm out walking. It's one of the few places free from distractions and a chance to simply sit and reflect."

Katie's brows scrunched together and her eyes widened. She looked perplexed before suggesting there were other places more conducive to reflection: a park bench, a house of worship, the library, a cushy chair in a bookstore, even a coffee shop. I told her those were good ideas but that I wasn't much of an expensive coffee drinker, hadn't attended shul in half a century, fell asleep in cushy chairs, and didn't know of a nice park that wasn't filled with noisy children.

"I like it here. There's a familiarity and dull sameness that works for me."

For several weeks, I continued to stop, sit and watch before Dr. Chan appeared and took the seat next to mine. He had a look of practiced, youthful concern acquired during medical school rounds when doctors-in-training knew a little but were expected to know a lot. Given my age and experience and, without any formal training, I know a bit about human nature. I sensed from his stiff posture and eyes that looked away from mine that he was struggling to be confrontive. I thought I'd save him the trouble.

"Katie is a nice addition to the waiting room. There's a perkiness about her that I appreciate very much. I'll bet she has reported a concern about my sitting here day after day. Well, I'm not here every day, but I do drop in frequently."

Dr. Chan now looked directly into my eyes with his jaw set confidently. My statement had clarified his agenda and I knew his Stanford smarts would serve him well.

"I'm happy you like Katie. She is very professional and she did mention a concern over how much time you are spending in the waiting room. Is everything okay with you? You don't have another appointment for several months."

"I'm fine, Dr. Chan. This is a good stop when I'm out on my morning walk. I don't come by during my afternoon walk. There's no need for any concern."

Dr. Chan nodded with understanding and a quiet assurance that he probably gives all of his more ancient patients before saying, "Well, it's good that you are getting regular exercise. There's nothing better than a good walk. Feel free to ask Katie for water if you need any."

I pointed to the canteen on my hip and thanked Dr. Chan for his support. He stood, walked over to Katie's window, leaned forward and in a low voice assured her that all was well with me. He turned and smiled back at me before going back to the examination rooms. I smiled back at Katie, gave an abbreviated salute, and told her how much I valued her concern. That's when a young boy with six fingers on his left hand walked in with his mom and dad.

2

Wink

I remember meeting Mr. Seymour when I was seven years old. For the five years I knew him, I always called him Mr. Seymour even though he always insisted on Sy. It was when my father had an appointment with his dermatologist and my mother and I sat with him in a waiting room while this older man sat across from us. The first thing I noticed was that he held a green canteen and was taking slow sips while his eyes seem to wander about the room before he spotted us. I had never seen a canteen before and, when I pointed at it with my left hand, he said it was Army surplus. He explained that it was a lot more useful than the popular over-priced plastic and glass water containers.

"It was made to go through a war and is virtually indestructible. Much more practical than the junk they sell these days while trying to guilt you into not purchasing water in plastic, throwaway containers. Would you like to take a closer look?"

I looked at my dad for approval and he nodded okay. Mr. Seymour patted the chair next to him, waited for me to sit, and handed me the canteen. It had a few dents and the screw top was attached to the body with a short chain, which I thought was a really good idea. I handed it back and returned to the seat between my parents.

My dad was called and he walked through the door to the right of the reception desk to the examination room. He was having a dark spot on his forearm checked out and told me it was nothing to worry about. Dad was good about reminding me to not worry about things. He had a way of describing anything that was unusual or unique as being a gift. He always told me that the extra finger on my left hand made me special and that being different was a blessing. It took me well into my adulthood before I understood what he meant.

I looked at Mr. Seymour and saw someone who was different, too. He was a small man, elfin like, and dressed as though he was going to a track meet. He wore a red beret that seemed to be having difficulty holding down a curly mass of white hair. His face was smooth and closely shaved with bushy brows and a shiny, straight nose. His red Vans, which at age seven I found amusing, were hardly scuffed. His eyes might have been blue or green and were focused on my left hand. I think he was trying to count my fingers without being overly obvious.

Finally, I held out both my hands and said with a bit too much force, "One has six fingers."

My mother pulled my left hand back and chastised me saying, "Wink, that's not polite. Say you're sorry."

Before I could say anything, Mr. Seymour interjected, "That's really all right. I'm afraid I was the one being impolite. I'm the one who should be sorry. It's a rare treat to see something different these days. The world has become so homogenized. My name is Seymour but you can call me Sy."

Mr. Seymour leaned across and held out his hand to shake mine. I felt pride when shaking his hand with my five-fingered hand because he saw me as a "rare treat." I didn't know what he meant by "homogenized" but it sounded like a good thing.

"So, your name is Wink," he said holding out his left hand. "Let's shake left-handed. It will be a first for me."

I thought it was the nicest thing a stranger could possibly do. I felt like a famous person and gave his hand an extra wiggle from my two middle fingers. He chuckled and said how nice it was to meet me. I told him my real name was Tony but that my parents nicknamed me Wink because my father had taught me to wink before I even learned to talk.

"Are you here to see Dr. Chan, too?" I asked. My mother again said it was impolite to ask such a question, but Mr. Seymour replied that it was okay. He said Dr. Chan was one of his doctors, but he was not there to see him on that day.

"I like to stop in during my daily walk and sit for a bit, thinking. I once read about some people who pay a lot of money to be put into some sort of sensory deprivation tank so that they can ease their worries and anxiety. They float in warm water in a completely dark tank without sound or other distractions. I guess it's like being back in their mother's womb. Weird I'd say. I find this waiting room to be infinitely boring and an affordable version of sensory deprivation."

I looked at my mother without a clue to what Mr. Seymour was talking about. She smiled and shrugged her shoulders acknowledging that she, too, was clueless. Mr. Seymour attempted to clarify, "What I mean is that this is a good place to relax." As it turns out, this would be the first of many days trying to understand Mr. Seymour.

I heard my father's voice behind the closed door. He was making a follow-up appointment. He told my mother that Dr. Chan wanted to remove the spot on his arm and it would be a minor surgical procedure. He used a word that caused my mother to blanch.

"Dr. Chan says not to worry till after it's biopsied. If it's malignant, there are lots of successful treatments."

Two weeks later, the spot was excised, tested, and later reported to be benign. That was also the second day I saw Mr. Seymour. My parents were as surprised as I when we walked into the waiting room and saw him sitting in the same chair as before and wearing the same outfit. While my father was being attended to, I asked Mr. Seymour about his beret and red Vans. Of course, my mother reminded me for the umpteenth time that I was not being respectful by being so nosy. Mr. Seymour smiled and said it was okay. I hadn't seen him smile so broadly during our first meeting and his teeth looked much too large for such a small man. Maybe they weren't real, but I knew not to mention it.

"I wear a beret for that jaunty appearance. It puts others at ease, sometimes amuses them, and gives me a flash of sophistication. The Vans were a closeout deal and the most comfortable shoes I've ever worn."

He had used several words new to my vocabulary, well above a seven-year old's. I figured he was just being funny and let the meaning go. I didn't have any grandparents in my life and he had the potential to become one.

My mother asked, "Do you live nearby, Mr. Seymour?"

"Not too far. I'm at the Vision of Eden. It's supposed to be a good place for active seniors. I'm active but not with the other old folks. They all seem a little too inactive for me. And you?" he asked.

"We're actually very close. We're in the neighborhood just across the boulevard from you. I'm surprised we haven't bumped into you outside of this waiting room."

"I don't usually cross the boulevard on my walks. What do you do when you're not here waiting for you husband?"

"I have a dog walking business. It keeps me busy while Wink is at school. My husband is a stone mason. And you, Mr. Seymour?"

Now, I thought my mother was being the nosy one. But mother used her mellow dog walker's voice, which demanded a dog's attention and now Mr. Seymour's. My mother had a way with tone and the economy of words.

"It's a long story. Needless to say, I'm now retired and enjoy walking."

"Where do you walk on Saturdays? This waiting room is not open."

"Saturdays are days for aimless walking. I never have a plan."

"Perhaps you'd like to join Wink and me when we walk our dog. Afterall, we are just across the boulevard from Visions. By the way, my name is Sylvie Mills."

"And mine is Seymour S. Seymour. I'm sure you can surmise what the S stands for. My parents had a wonderful sense of humor. But, please, call me Sy."

I stood and enthusiastically chimed in, "Yes, yes Mr. Seymour. It would be great to walk with you. My dog Rex is the best dog. He's kind of like me. He's different. He only has three legs. He's what they call a tripod."

"I'd like to walk with you and Rex. Where shall we meet?"

This began five years of Saturday walks with Mr. Seymour and Rex until both of them passed on shortly after Mr. Seymour celebrated his 90th birthday and I my 12th.

3

Sylvie

When I married Mel, Rex was part of the deal. I had recently adopted Rex from a friend who bred standard poodles. Rex was born a tripod, missing his right front leg, unsalable but giftable. The good thing about dogs is that they have no conception of their own mortality or limitations. Rex was a romper who enjoyed fetching and snuggling. Before long, he was a certified therapy dog who enjoyed comforting children, adults, and other dogs. There were even a few neighborhood cats who took a liking to Rex. Rex was born a puppy who was emotionally well beyond his puppy years. His black coat shimmered and his deep black eyes held their gaze as long as it took to be offered a beef jerky snack. Mel insisted that Rex be the ring bearer at our wedding and have a prominent place at the reception dinner table.

Rex was two when our eleven-fingered Wink was born. Mel thought it fitting that Wink and Rex both possessed a quality that made them unique. He believed that difference was a strength, which, when understood and embraced, made for a stronger, more compassionate person. I began my dog walking business when Wink went off to kindergarten. Two years later, we met Mr. Seymour, another unique person who would change all of our lives.

The first Saturday Mr. Seymour accompanied us for a walk, I retrieved a leather leash and announced, "Rex, it's time to go to work. Wink, you're coming along, too. I think Mr. Seymour would like you to walk with both of us."

Rex trotted over and sat with his eyes fixed on me as I clipped the leash to his collar. Rex had a temperament that calmed other dogs. He was the perfect walking companion for some of the more anxious and excitable dogs on my client list. Jasmine, an impetuous and demanding Yorkshire terrier, behaved herself as soon as Rex, waiting stoically and patiently at my side, cocked his head indicating it was time to walk. Jasmine complied and dutifully strutted alongside Rex for our fifteen-minute walk. The German Shepard Gunther, a rescue from a shelter that abused animals, growled and showed signs of aggression in unfamiliar surroundings. When walking with Rex, Gunther learned to restrain his off-putting behavior from the modeling of Rex's even demeanor, especially when encountering strangers along the way. In our first days walking together, Gunther would shy away and growl menacingly when strangers approached. Over time, as Gunther watched Rex accept friendly pats and treats from others, he allowed strangers to scratch him behind his upturned ears without being reactive. Rex and I worked three hours in the morning and repeated another three in the afternoon. Most of the time, we walked two or three dogs at once. Jasmine and Gunther, because of their special needs, were the few who had individual walks. On Saturdays, we only walked three dogs in the morning. They were what I referred to as "special needs" dogs because they required individual attention from both Rex and me. Wink usually walked with us on Saturdays unless Mel had a father/son activity planned. On the Saturday Mr. Seymour was going to join us, we had already walked two dogs when, right on schedule, there was Mr. Seymour waiting at a predetermined corner. Wink, Rex, and I approached with Chili, an overly determined dachshund who had a propensity for uncontrolled barking. Rex would immediately close the distance between himself and Chili; the barking would cease and not resume until Chili was back home.

Mr. Seymour waved and indicated he'd cross the street. He strode toward us with the bounce of a much younger man. He wore his usual sweats, canteen attached to the Army belt, a red beret I found slightly comical sitting atop his unruly, gray hair, and the red Vans that Wink told me were the best shoes ever. I preferred my New Balance tennis shoes because they were made in America and Mel and I try to buy only American. It's not that we were being patriotic or politically correct, whatever that means; rather, we like to buy local as much as we can. We're not even sure why. We initially thought it was better for the environment and more supportive of homegrown businesses. Shopping at our local food co-op began as a commitment to buying organic, but now it's just a habit. I find it funny how habits begin with purpose and morph to unexplainable routines, regardless of the expense.

"It's nice to see you on this lovely Saturday morning. You have two nice looking pooches to walk with us," said Mr. Seymour as he reached out with his left hand to shake Wink's six-fingered hand, which Wink found to be extraordinarily kind.

I said, "Good of you to join us Mr. Seymour. We'll walk Chili for about fifteen or twenty minutes and, if you'd like, we can walk some more after we return her home."

"Please, call me Sy. I'm up for walking as long as you and Wink want to. I miss walking with a doggy companion."

"You had a dog?" asked Wink.

"Oh, yes, Tony was a scruffy thing. He was about the size of Chili, brown and white, with wiry hair and a mutt's need for constant attention. We were definitely the best of pals. It's been a long time since he passed."

"Gee, Tony is my real name," gushed Wink.

"What a happy coincidence," said Mr. Seymour.

Mr. Seymour went on to tell of all the dogs, cats, turtle, rabbits, hamsters, and various other pets he and his wife had with their three sons. He told me that Tony was his last pet and, after his wife died, he insisted that his oldest grandson take him.

"I needed quiet time and couldn't manage an active pup. It's certainly a pleasure to be walking with you, Wink, and the dogs. Really nice," he said with sincere appreciation. "Now, I live in a very nice senior residence, take daily walks, and maybe this will become a regular Saturday walk. I hope you don't mind the suggestion."

I didn't mind it at all. Saturday walks with Mr. Seymour became a regular habit. It didn't take long before I invited him over for Saturday suppers. For five years, Saturday walks and dinners with Mr. Seymour became a fixture in our lives. Despite his insistence on being called Sy, he remained Mr. Seymour to us. I felt that his quirky dignity demanded the formality. I wanted Wink to grow up respectful of an older generation.

We dropped off Chili and began our return to the corner where we met Mr. Seymour on that first of many Saturday walks. We extended the walk by taking an indirect route back to the corner by weaving through some of the surrounding neighborhood streets. It was our neighborhood, a community of modest homes. Wink asked Mr. Seymour if he still walked to the doctor's waiting room and he said almost every day. I asked if he ever walked with others, friends or family. He said his sons all lived in other states, although they frequently stayed in touch with phone calls and video chats.

"I have a few friends, but they're not walkers. Mostly, they like to go for coffee or lunch when they go out. And they rarely go out."

"Have you always been a walker, Mr. Seymour?" I asked.

"No. I was really more of a sitter before I retired. Even in my free time, I sat around and watched too much television. My wife got me walking and I've kept it up. I'm eighty-five and I feel like I have a lot more walking in me."

Wink suggested that Mr. Seymour keep track of his steps with a pedometer. But Mr. Seymour suggested that randomness was more interesting than predictability.

"The whole world has become one big data gathering and spewing machine. Everything needs to be measured. I find the unmeasurable to be much more intriguing."

I could tell from the look on Wink's face that he had no idea what Mr. Seymour was saying. I'm not sure I understood, either.

I asked, "What do you mean by 'unmeasurable'?"

Mr. Seymour stopped walking, looked at Wink and me, and paused before speaking. I came to know him as a pauser. He exuded thoughtfulness and patience. I recalled him saying one time how he used the waiting room's blandness to 'sit and reflect.'

"Well, I don't really believe in an all-knowing spirit, a divine spirit of any sort, but I do feel very spiritual when looking at what I call 'unmeasurables.' For instance, how do you measure the sweet scent of roses, the beauty of a sunset, or the feeling you get when holding your grandchild. I'm sure someone has come up with some sort of quantifiable measure, but I'm not sure sensory experiences are quantifiable, even on a one to ten scale."

Wink continued to look confused with tightened lips and brows. I nodded and told Mr. Seymour that I now understood. We finished our walk and Mr. Seymour insisted that Wink give him that extra two middle-finger wiggle with their left-handed shake. Wink couldn't help but smile and laugh with a twinkle in his eye.

"Now, that's what I call an unmeasurable," said Mr. Seymour as he saluted a goodbye.

4

Mel

I really didn't notice Mr. Seymour when I had my initial appointment with Dr. Chan. I was more concerned about the dark spot that had recently appeared on my left forearm and had difficulty paying attention to anything else. When my son Wink asked me for permission look at Mr. Seymour's beat-up Army surplus canteen, I briefly snapped out of the spell of self-pity I had put myself under. I generally keep a positive outlook even when faced with significant problems. Usually, they are other folk's problems and I'm good at dispensing advice while keeping an emotional distance. Now, I couldn't help thinking about whether or not that dark spot was skin cancer. I always thought a melanoma was a death sentence.

I work as a stone mason. Most days I'm laboring under a hot sun building brick facades, forming block foundations, or erecting stone retaining walls. I like my job. Every day I can see the fruits of my labor. When a job is finished, I take pride in pointing out what I did to my wife Sylvie and my son Wink. My work is all about adding structure, yet here I was believing some of my own structure was about to be removed. Would I lose an arm? Would I have a noticeable physical difference like our eleven-fingered son Wink or our tripod dog Rex? Would I be able to continue doing the work that allowed us to live a comfortable life?

In that brief moment when I gave the okay for Wink to sit with Mr. Seymour, I observed an old man who seemed to have a calm and gentle demeanor. It's hard to describe how I came to that opinion. It wasn't anything he said, because he had yet to say much. It wasn't any sort of aura, because I don't believe in auras. I think it was about his nonchalant appearance. It was clear from his attire that he dressed for himself and not others. Who wears a red beret and shockingly red sneakers when you are clearly past the age of youthful garb? His nonverbal ease with himself, and I thought a comical outlook, put me at ease with my own unknown circumstance.

My appointment with Dr. Chan was the first time in my life I would need to make a medical decision about myself. It was much easier to make a medical decision about Wink when he was a newborn. Shortly after Wink was born, my wife Sylvie and I were asked to decide about our son's extra finger on his left hand. The medical staff had advised that polydactyly was a rare birth anomaly easily corrected through surgical removal of the extra digit. In this case, the extra digit was between his middle and ring finger. It was the same length as his middle finger, essentially giving him two middle fingers. The doctors advised that early removal was best and we should decide as soon as possible. The surgeon who was a member of the team joked that it would be no more traumatic than the circumcision we had already scheduled. It felt like he saw our son's extra finger as an easily solved cosmetic issue, rather than one with bigger consequences. I had heard of others who lost limbs from trauma or amputation and suffered from mysterious pains. I think they were called phantom pains. Would our son have lifelong pain due to a surgically removed digit? Sylvie and I were taken aback by the surgeon's cavalier attitude and did not appreciate his condescending smile when he appeared to speak through us, as though we were invisible parents who did not know what was best for our newborn son. We asked if there was anything wrong with the extra finger and were told that it appeared to be a fully functioning digit and not like the more common stubby and poorly formed extension of extra tissue, which served no practical use and might be off-putting to others.

Sylvie asked, "What do you think we should do, Mel?"

"It seems that our son has been born with a difference, just like Rex. And you know I believe that difference makes us stronger. I think this is an easy choice. We should leave things as they are."

Sylvie and I had heard stories from friends and family that the first thing you do after giving birth is count fingers and toes to make sure all is well. We were surprised by Wink's extra finger, but not dismayed. It did cause us to rethink baby names. The ones we had already selected didn't seem to fit. We left the hospital and returned home with unnamed Baby Mills assuring the hospital administrator we would call as soon as we came up with a name that fit. It took a few minutes of online research before we named our son Tony, not Anthony, after a famous baseball pitcher who also sported an extra digit.

We adored our firstborn, and, as it turned out, our only child.

From his very first days, I greeted Tony with a broad grin and a wink while giving an exaggerated lift of my bushy eyebrows. Sylvie smiled whenever I held Tony in my large, callused hands and said, "How's my boy today?" It wasn't long before Tony began to mimic me by smiling back with his glistening dark green eyes, raising his eyebrows, and winking back. I began prompting Tony with "show me a Groucho" and Tony would lift his brows and wink.

Sylvie found Tony's quick ability to copy my funny-facing joyful and a sign of Tony's intelligence. Tony began winking and giggling in approval when being fed, nuzzled, and tickled, and we nicknamed him Wink. Tony "Wink" Mills was a shy and slightly introverted boy. When Wink told me how special he felt when Mr. Seymour requested they shake left hands, I knew Mr. Seymour would be a positive influence on my son. When Wink turned nine, he asked for red tennis shoes and a red beret. He wore them proudly till he turned twelve.

I wish I learned more about Mr. Seymour during the five years he was in our lives. I'm not one to pry. Sylvie thinks asking personal questions is discourteous. Wink, on the other hand and despite his shyness, had no trouble asking Mr. Seymour any question that popped into his young mind: Where did you grow up? What were your parents like? How did you meet your wife? Are you still sad about her dying? Don't you ever get to see your kids? Do you like being a grandfather? Why do you wear the same clothes all the time? And on and on they came. Mr. Seymour always listened earnestly and answered sincerely.

Wink saved me from asking the one question I would have liked to ask. I had joined them on one of their Saturday walks when Wink asked, "Mr. Seymour, what's your first name?"

"It's Seymour. My full name is Seymour S. Seymour, and don't ask what the S stands for. My parents had a warped sense of humor."

I couldn't hold back a laugh, a rather loud one-syllable, hiccup of a laugh. Sylvie looked over at me with a how-could-you expression.

Mr. Seymour smiled with all his large teeth and said, "Yep, a warped sense of humor."

Wink quickly responded, "Your name is Seymour Seymour Seymour. How cool is that!"

"It's very cool, but please call me Sy."

I apologized for laughing. Mr. Seymour said that was okay and, in fact, it was the whole point of his name. He added, "It took me a while before I realized my parents' wry humor was a gift. I don't know if they realized how much it helped me to become comfortable with myself. I used my strange, comical name as a way of putting others at ease. When

I was a teenager, I went by S.S. Seymour and told my friends that, like Harry S Truman's middle initial, the S.S. stood for nothing. I doubt they believed me, but it did get a good laugh. In my professional life, my name was proudly highlighted on my calling card. It garnered attention, and in my profession attention was important. In new social situations, my name became an ice breaker. I never thought of changing my name because it became an important asset in my daily life."

Mr. Seymour made me think about the intended or unintended consequences of what Sylvie and I did as parents. We were both very happy that we nicknamed our son Wink.

5

Lights Out

Wink turned twelve a few months before Seymour celebrated his ninetieth birthday at the Visions of Eden Home for Active Seniors. Wink and Seymour walked together on one of those rare Saturday occasions when Sylvie had no dogs to walk. Seymour walked with a briskness few ninety-year-old men were capable of, and Wink sometimes labored to keep up. Wink had reached an age when he could appreciate Seymour's good health and insightful conversation. In fact, it was a few weeks before Wink's twelfth birthday and Seymour noticed that Wink had stopped wearing his red beret and red tennis shoes in exchange for an orange hoodie and black Converse high-tops.

Seymour immediately commented on Wink's fresh appearance, "It's important to find your own voice through deed and symbolism."

"I get what you mean by 'deed.' My dad is always talking about the importance of doing good work. I'm not sure what you mean by symbolism."

Seymour, as he was apt to do, paused, touched his hand to his chin, and replied, "Deeds and actions make noise, but symbols are quiet representations of who we are. It's important that deeds and symbols don't conflict with one another."

Wink was always fascinated by Seymour's philosophizing. He imagined that there was more to what he said than he would ever understand. Sometimes, it was like listening to a sage's whispers when Seymour spoke, and it demanded Wink's attention.

Wink and his parents had been invited to Seymour's milestone birthday. Sylvie and Mel talked about what it might be like to live so long. Wink wondered if Seymour thought about how much time he had to live, was he afraid of dying, and did he think about whether or not there was a god and life after death. He didn't waste any time asking Seymour the next time they went for a walk, and it wasn't hard for Seymour to respond.

It was an early summer day. Wink was on summer vacation from school and found new opportunities to accompany Seymour on one of his regular walks. This meant a stop at what Seymour described as the "beige, boring, waiting room only fit for rest and introspection." Wink found Seymour's walking routines and his stop for quiet reflection amusing, yet important. The day was filled with sunshine and a moderate temperature. Seymour wore his lightweight sweatsuit along with a new pair of red Vans and his customary red beret, which was beginning to fray around the edges. Wink quietly made a mental note to tell his mother a new beret might be a perfect birthday gift.

Before arriving at the medical offices, Seymour surprised Wink by asking a question. Wink had been trying to find the right words to ask his own questions and was taken off guard when Seymour asked him if he understood how lucky he was to have two middle fingers on his left hand. For five years, Seymour insisted they shake left hands at the beginning and end of their walks, with Wink being sure to wiggle his two middle fingers in Seymour's palm.

"Lucky?" asked Wink.

"Yes, lucky," replied Seymour. "Well, I guess I'm really the lucky one," added Seymour. "When we shake hands, I feel joy and a special bond. You are like another grandson to me."

"You're like family to us, too."

Katie, the receptionist who always wore bright colors and a neutral affect, welcomed Seymour and Wink before they took seats in the far corner of the waiting room. There were two others seated apart and across the room who looked at them with obvious curiosity. Wink could hear one whisper to the other, "he's wearing a beret," and wondered if either would eventually notice his left hand. Wink, not having his younger impetuous nature when he'd blurt out a question to his mother's chagrin, considered how to ask Seymour about life and death.

"Mr. Seymour, you are about to be ninety. I've been wondering if you think much about the end of life. What do you think it means to die?" The two across the room became quiet and looked to Wink and Seymour with anticipation.

Without hesitating, which was unusual for Seymour he said, "That's a very good question and I'm glad you asked."

He told Wink that he had once read a book or an article somewhere, or maybe heard from another resident at the retirement home, about what

Steve Jobs said about dying. Jobs thought life was like having an on-and-off switch and that once you're done, you're done. Jobs said he wasn't all that concerned about the end of life.

"I'm focused on living. When my time is up, it's up," said Seymour with a calm reassurance. "Of course, if there is anything beyond, I'll happily welcome the extension."

Wink had little understanding or concern with mortality. Although he was a precocious twelve-year-old who earned the highest grades in school and had a special proclivity for mathematics, the fuzzier aspects of life were not easily grasped. It would be much later, as a middle-aged adult with a wife and three children, when he would obsess over life's limits. That was when he recalled Seymour's nonchalance with death and wished he might have a similar attitude. He didn't share his fears with anyone, not even his wife. Rather, he wondered how much longer he would be clipping his fingernails and toenails? How many more haircuts he'd have in his lifetime? When would brushing his teeth come to an end? Would he live to be ninety like Seymour before finding comfort with the unknown?

Shortly before Seymour's birthday party, Wink had taken to wearing a bolo tie with a Western-style shirt and a belt featuring a garish, silver-colored belt buckle in the shape of a horseshoe. Seymour complimented him on seeking his own voice and unique style.

"I like your style, Wink. I look forward to your next experimentation."

He looks forward, thought Wink. There wasn't an ounce of nostalgia in Seymour. The stories about his family were always in the present tense.

"What was your wife like?" asked Wink.

"She is the best. The best cook. The best mother. The best wife. She will always be the best."

"Were you kids into sports?"

"My oldest son plays soccer with my grandchildren."

Seymour turned the past into the now.

A few months after his ninetieth birthday, Seymour was diagnosed with a severe respiratory illness. His breathing was labored and he stopped taking long walks. He spent most of his days at the retirement home, either sitting in the solarium with a few friends or asleep in his room. Wink would frequently visit after school on his way home. His parents encouraged him to spend as much time as he could with Seymour, and they would often drop by with some of Seymour's favorite snacks, fig Newton cookies. In time, Wink would become a fan of fig Newtons and savor them one small bite at a time just like Seymour.

Unlike Seymour always being in the present or looking to the future, Wink thought a lot about the five years spent with his adopted grandfather. Never once had he called him Sy, even with Seymour's nudging not to be so formal. It was always Mr. Seymour. He would always be grateful for left-handed shakes and the acceptance of all things different. Seymour disdained chain stores, anything that was franchised, and what he called the "homogenization of place." It took a while, but Wink finally began to understand Seymour's declarations of preferences.

During Wink's last visit to the Visions of Eden Home for Active Seniors, Seymour was sitting up in bed reading Klara and the Sun. Wink asked him if it was a good book. Seymour said he was enjoying it very much, and that it seemed to be about what it meant to be human. He told Wink it was different from the other Ishiguro books he had read.

"He's such a fantastic writer. I hope you'll read him when you are a little older and able to fully grasp what he says in his books. This book paints a pretty scary future, but I think it's good for us to confront possibilities."

Wink and Seymour spoke for a while and ate a few fig Newtons. Seymour's breathing seemed more labored than during recent visits. He had developed an echoey wheeze, which disturbed Wink.

Wink stood to leave and Seymour asked him to turn off the light. Just before flipping the light switch from on to off, Wink said, "I love you, Sy."

6

Pinky

Flora came into our lives as Tinker Bell. We adopted her after Wink's mother, an occasional dog-walker for friends, explained that her owner had become too old to care for her. Unlike the character in Peter Pan for whom she was named, there was nothing sassy about her at all. She was a calm, cuddly four-year-old Norwich terrier with a disposition to please, which was contrary to being a typical terrier. Belly rubs, fingers running through her wiry reddish fur and an occasional jerky treat was what she favored. Wink and I named her Flora as a companion to Fauna, a comical black and white mutt we found abandoned in front of the Stop and Go market. We took Fauna home after the store manager told us she had been tied to the newspaper rack for over two days.

"I've been feeding, watering, and walking her, but I can't let her in the store and my girlfriend is allergic so I can't bring her in the house. She stays in the garage at night, doesn't make a sound. I don't have the heart to drop her at the animal shelter. She's quiet and likes it when I walk her in the woods behind the store."

We named her Fauna, gave her a good long bath when we got her home and watched her personality emerge. The vet said she was a five- or six-year-old, part this and part that. She had the deep chested body of a Lab, a Dalmatian's skinny legs, Bassett Hound eyes, uneven black fur, and the coordination of a clumsy Buster Keaton. She was like someone had tried rolling the dice for a Yahtzee but came up with a Chance instead. When Flora joined the family, Fauna blossomed from a slightly withdrawn and tentative dog to a more engaging and playful companion. They were inseparable and Flora, being half Fauna's size and three-times as coordinated, became a constant twosome rolling around on the floor and playing tug with a variety of toys. Little did we know that Flora and Fauna would become critical companions and comforters during the most stressful time in our future family.

Wink and I were also inseparable. We met when he came into the clinic for a blood test, where I worked as a phlebotomist. He was completing an insurance physical for a job at the local community college. When he noticed my name tag "Sylvia Kline," he commented that his mother's name was Sylvie.

"It's an old-fashioned name for a new-age girl," I replied whenever someone commented on my name. I wasn't a fan of my own name, but because of Jewish tradition, I had been named after my Great Aunt Sima. "It's a family thing," I explained. "What arm would you like for the blood draw?"

He rolled up his left arm's sleeve and that's when I noticed the six perfectly manicured fingers. I prepped his arm, drew blood, affixed a happy-face band aid, and instructed him to return to the waiting room where he would be called for the remainder of his physical. I can't really explain what happened next.

I am not an impetuous person. My friends describe me as a careful planner, a scheduler, as someone averse to surprises. I might take hours making to-do lists for short- and long-term activities. It is common to be told to 'get on with it' when considering what to wear or when selecting the perfect lemon at the grocery store. I don't make snap judgments. It would be a long process before I decided whether or not a current boyfriend was the right boyfriend. I tend toward over-forgivingness.

It wasn't just noticing his six-fingered left hand that caused me to blurt out what I said with a sense of immature embarrassment. I'm sure I was influenced by the handprinted name on his paperwork, "Wink Mills," which was different from the computer-generated label that said, "Tony Mills." I supposed that Wink was a preferred nickname. I was also attracted to his smile, cleft chin, dimpled cheeks when he smiled, and green eyes, which communicated a soft, penetrating warmth. It was also the way he dressed. He wore a red beret and red Vans. Before he showed up at the clinic and sat in the chair at my lab station, I didn't have a nickname. I had never thought about having a nickname. Even though my given same Sylvia could easily have been shortened to Sylvie, as I later learned like Wink's mother Sylvie, it wasn't. Even my middle name Gertrude, given in tribute to another great aunt, could have been shortened to Gertie or Trudie. I was always Sylvia, or when my mother was angry with me Sylvia Gertrude. But in that moment, after counting his six beautiful fingers, noticing Wink written on the lab form, and drawing blood from his left arm, I said without any immediate understanding of where it came from, "You can call me Pinky."

"Is it a color preference? Or an aversion to being called Thumbs because in your line of work you wouldn't want to be referred to as all thumbs. Right? And Pinky seems to go along with being a phlebotomist. Doesn't it? Or might it be the fact that you don't usually encounter a six-fingered man on a daily basis? It's okay because being different is okay."

His comeback to my impulsive silliness didn't seem rehearsed, argumentative, and without any expectation of a response. How does someone come up with quick, spontaneous replies, which I would never be capable of? It felt genuine without being contemptuous. I felt my cheeks flush and didn't know how to respond. I'm sure he noticed my unease. He reached out with his right hand and touched my forearm with an empathetic gesture to my awkwardness.

"It's okay. I go by Wink. It's a long story. If I were Winky we'd rhyme. Perhaps we could meet after your shift and talk about this unique similarity?"

I knew it was a pick-up line. I was accustomed to those. I'm not an unattractive woman. I work out for an hour every morning at the Y before work, the rowing machine, spinning, swimming laps. My body is toned and agile. I wear my auburn hair in a convenient mannish cut. I use moisturizer and my skin is smooth and unblemished. I know my smile is inviting because my mother always said that my smile was an opening to conversation. I eat healthy due to my best friend who is a dietician at the clinic and who always gifts me a weekly menu of good eats, which I try to follow with the exception of Brussels sprouts, calves liver, or an inordinate amount of beans.

"Okay, I'll meet you for dinner. Dutch treat. First, I need to know if you'll be wearing the red beret and sneakers. That could be a deal breaker if you are as quirky as you present. And I'm not apologizing for being cautious or inappropriately forward."

"Well, Pinky," he said. "Even though I believe you just made up your nickname, which, by the way, I think is fitting and extraordinarily cute, I'm wearing the hat and shoes in tribute to a dear friend who died fifteen years ago today. I wear the outfit on the anniversary of his death. Seymour was a special person. It's a long, beautiful story, which I'll be happy to tell you over dinner."

I thought about the yahrzeit candles my family lit on the anniversaries of our relatives deaths and on Yom HaShoah, Holocaust Remembrance Day. Wink had a specialness about him. He was aware that I was faking it with my just-invented nickname, was quick-witted without being mean-spirited, and was very handsome. His pick-up line worked.

He asked about my dinner preference and I said anything but barbecue. He suggested vegan and I told him I never ate vegan, gluten-free, paleo, or any other diet that had a history of going viral on social media. He said the suggestion was just a sanity test and that I passed.

"But no barbecue?" he asked.

"If you ever had my grandmother's brisket you'd understand."

Understanding food preferences was easy. Understanding unexpected tragedy was the hardest challenge to our lives. Our lives became entwined like ivy-covered walls. We learned to support each other, which became a vital necessity after tragedy. Wink and I married after dating for over a year. Although he grew up without any formal religion, our mutual secularism was all the faith we needed. My parents insisted on a Jewish marriage. Wink thought that would be great. His parents were happy with whatever we did but had two requests. Wink's father Mel wanted to contribute by building a chuppah for the ceremony. His mother Sylvie asked that their latest pet, a tripod standard poodle named Rex the Reincarnate, be the ring bearer. Flora and Fauna came into our lives shortly after we returned from our honeymoon. His mother delighted in having grand dogs and looked after them when Wink and I were at work.

Fourteen years later, we lived near both of our parents and had two sons. Seth is twelve and Boyd is nine. Boyd's twin sister Rose was two when she was killed, struck down by a bullet out of nowhere. Before we were married, and when Wink shared stories about Mr. Seymour, he told me that Mr. Seymour said death was nothing more than turning off a light switch. One moment you are on and the next off. Losing Rose was much more than turning off a light bulb. It was like a dimmer switch that continuously darkened our world with no end in sight. The dimness would not reverse into brighter times for almost a year.

So much slowly turned off. Except for the necessities of day-to-day life, we remained at home. Wink taught his classes but maintained office hours at home. Few students took advantage of his dourness. Fortunately, he had an understanding dean. I continued to work at the clinic, while giving up all the volunteer time I gave to various community events. Wink would always be Wink, but it would be a while before I could be Pinky again. I was just Sylvia for now. The boys were two and five. Wink's mother cared for Boyd and the dogs while I was at work. Seth was in an extended-day kindergarten taught by Mrs. Gillespie, who became a second mother to him. Boyd and Seth knew their sister was gone forever but had no understanding of forever.

Unlike historical tragedies told in books and plays, personal tragedy happens without any preface. It was cool Autumn Saturday and Rose was playing in the front yard when she suddenly and soundlessly collapsed on the freshly mowed lawn. She was small for her age and her curly, brown hair sprung in multiple directions giving her the illusion of being in perpetual motion. She would kick her red, rubber ball around the fenced yard for hours. No doubt she had the makings of a future soccer star. I was sitting on the front porch enjoying my mid-morning coffee and watching my toddling daughter amuse herself with the beginnings of understandable speech as she talked to the ball with her own invented language. Flora and Fauna sat next to me while keeping their eyes on Rose. They were not enamored with two-year-old energy but were attentive companions. I cherished Saturdays. Wink was inside watching some silly morning cartoons with the boys.

When Rose fell, I thought she had simply stumbled from running so hard. Flora and Fauna sensed something was wrong and leapt off the porch and ran to her side. When she didn't stand or utter a sound for what seemed like an immeasurable time, but was only seconds, I ran to her and saw the blood pooling from her chest. There had been no warning, I heard no sound, no crack, no sharp pop, nothing indicating a distant gunshot.

Weeks passed and we had no answers other than the police reporting that a bullet discharged from an unknown rifle had killed Rose. The police assumed it must have been an errant shot so far away that I didn't hear it. They questioned neighbors within a one-mile radius, and there were a few reports of what sounded like a firecracker but no sightings of a shooter. It seemed implausible that a bullet could come out of nowhere.

We buried Rose and sat shiva for a week. One of our parents stayed overnight insisting that we should not be alone. The boys slept at my parents after spending the day experiencing a solemn Jewish ritual. Wink's folks kept Flora and Fauna and said they'd tend to them until we were ready to have them back in our house. For a week, the house was filled with friends and neighbors offering condolences and casseroles. Seth's kindergarten teacher Mrs. Gillespie dropped by every afternoon and spent over an hour sitting with both boys, reading from storybooks, and offering consoling hugs.

While I grieved, I stopped noticing the details of our lives. However, at the next anniversary of Mr. Seymour's passing, I realized Wink was not honoring the time by wearing a red beret and Vans. I found him sitting on the front porch in the same chair I had been using when Rose was murdered by an assailant who would forever be unknown. It was a chair I no longer used and doubted that I would ever sit in again. Wink was weeping, tears flowing down his cheeks and his mouth quivering with sadness. I leaned over and wrapped my arms around him, smelling the freshness of his showered hair. I had no words, nothing comforting to say. I pulled myself closer to him.

"Mr. Seymour lived a long life. He was ready to let go and have his switched turned off. He had a history with many chapters, which he wrote himself. Rose had written no chapters," sobbed Wink with raspy gasps. "Mr. Seymour lived long enough to have routines. He lived long enough to have reflection. Now, we are left only to reflect on what Rose might have been. It's not fair that we are left with the imagination of what could have been."

I stood, pulled a matching porch chair next to Wink, sat and asked, "What do you think Mr. Seymour would say if he were here?"

"He told me that one of his grandchildren had died as an infant from some rare heart defect. I was probably around ten at the time and with a ten-year-old's wisdom repeated what I had heard, but never experienced. I echoed the 'life is not fair' quote I had heard many times from others who were trying to console loved ones. Mr. Seymour nodded thoughtfully, as he always did when listening, and then said something I'm just now figuring out. He said that fairness was something only the naïve care about. Growing older is the opportunity to embrace acceptance and forgiveness while celebrating whatever time we have on earth."

Our focus began to expand. Our lives had been like cameras that had been on maximum zoom and were finally drawing back to a wider angle. The pinpoint attention to shared tragedy eased itself back to include more normal attention to our children, our jobs, our extended families, each other, and our dogs. Family and friends didn't hang around as much or check in to see how we were doing. With each passing day, a sense of normalcy grew.

Wink said that Mr. Seymour rejected the idea of normal. "Mr. Seymour said normal was an illusion interrupted by reality, or vice versa. Deal with the reality and use normal as a pleasant diversion."

I often wondered how pre-teen Wink ever understood Mr. Seymour. Was Mr. Seymour a Socrates to Wink's Plato? I had never met Mr. Seymour, yet twenty years later he profoundly impacted our lives. I feel that he saved us in ways we'll never comprehend.

We unveiled Rose's gravestone on the one-year anniversary of her death. We were joined by our parents and a few close friends. Seth's former kindergarten teacher Mrs. Gillespie attended. Seth held her hand throughout a brief ceremony when we each placed stones on her gravestone. My parents recited a few prayers. The rest of us chose a quiet remembrance. Boyd wandered about the adjacent gravesites, climbing on nearby headstones as though they were climbing structures intended for play. I looked over to see him sitting atop a stone inscribed Louis Cohen, February 14, 1915—May 19, 2002. He had lived a good long life and, for some reason, I realized he was born on Valentine's Day and died on Malcolm X's birthday.

Boyd smiled back at me while swinging his heels against the headstone. Flora and Fauna sniffed around adjacent tombstones, occasionally pawing at interesting scents. I was reminded of Thomas Hardy's poem "Are You Digging on My Grave." Boyd was three years old and I would have thought that a year of sadness might have rubbed off on him. I smiled back at Boyd with genuine love at what struck me as a comic scene, which I supposed was part of life. There was no sense of mortality in youth and dogs. I looked over at Seth standing solemnly alongside his former teacher. What is the timeline for solemnity? I held Wink's six-fingered hand in mine.

7

Mrs. Gillespie

Red and white were her favorite colors. The entire perimeter of the white picket fence enclosing the front yard was woven in red and white roses. The flower boxes hanging from her front windows and bedding areas on either side of the front porch contained densely packed red and white hydrangeas, petunias, geraniums, impatiens, begonias, as well as an assortment of perennial green fillers. The wall paper in her kitchen was plaid, emphasizing the vibrancy of red and white. Every other room continued the red and white theme. Mrs. Gillespie minimized blue because she didn't want to be taken as a patriotic zealot or a xenophobe. She quietly despised those who wrapped themselves in Old Glory and shook their fists while holding bibles like self-righteous and self-serving politicos. She recalled reading a quote attributed to Sinclair Lewis about how Fascism would come to America wrapped in a flag and waving a cross. It was the source of her abhorrence to the current state of a divided culture, but it didn't keep her from enjoying two of the three colors of the flag.

Mrs. Gillespie arrived as a small baby and grew to be a tiny woman with a soft voice, which required careful listening when she spoke. And she was born looking old and remained that way her entire life. Hardly anyone noticed when she went prematurely gray before turning thirty. Her rimless glasses rested on a broad nose protecting blue crystalline eyes that were in constant, curious motion. She maintained a neutral smile, which communicated care and understanding. Her only whimsy was the red lipstick she frequently touched up using the packet of tissues kept in a purse meant to be carried by a much larger woman. She dressed conservatively in dresses, always sporting a high neckline and falling below her knees. Other than a jacket or sweater necessitated by the weather, the only other article of clothing she wore outside the house was a smock when teaching kindergarten. She was particularly proud of the many heavy white smocks that had become multi-colored as evidenced by years of children wiping their hands of finger paints, white paste, clay, and the other rudiments of kindergarten life. Through regular washings, the smocks became the softest articles of clothing known to her students. They were like Snoopy security blankets. After nearly forty years of teaching, several smocks had been auctioned at the annual PTA fundraiser to former students who wished to pass them along to their children or grandchildren who were now in Mrs. Gillespie's charge.

Mrs. Gillespie had no children of her own. She and Mr. Gillespie married when she turned thirty and divorced nine years later just before turning forty. It was a marriage of impetuous spontaneity built on friendship and a pact that they would marry by a certain age if they had not found other life partners. The day following her thirtieth birthday, they took an early morning flight to Las Vegas, hailed a taxi from the airport to the Little White Wedding Chapel, and were married by an overly enthusiastic officiant with witnesses who were next-in-line for their own ceremony. They purchased the economy wedding picture package, took a taxi back to the airport, won seventy-six dollars in quarters playing the slots while waiting for their flight back home, and informed their friends families of their adventure. None seemed surprised about the marriage, but Mrs. Gillespie's mother wondered why she changed her last name. Mrs. Gillespie said her maiden name Finkelstein was too distracting.

"I'd rather the children call me Mrs. G rather than Mrs. F."

"Why would you say that?" asked her mother.

"I suppose Mrs. F sounds like a failure, but Mrs. G reminds me of glee. F is the beginning of so many bad words, four letter words, not the least of which is fool. But G is an encouraging letter like good, gracious, glad, grateful, and gorgeous."

"I think you're meshuga! But I'll love you anyway."

Mr. and Mrs. Gillespie didn't think of their marriage as crazy. In retrospect, they both realized their union was more about liking rather than loving each other. They enjoyed each other's company without intimacy. Communication was their bond. Conversations about family, work and neighborhood held them together. Once in a while they ventured into politics but found the topic unsavory at the Federal level and frustrating at the local. They rarely discussed religion except when someone began spouting hateful religious doctrine, which served to blame, intimidate, and label non-believers as satanic. Mrs. Gillespie was raised a reformed Jew by parents who participated in frequent streetcorner demonstrations supporting women's rights and animal causes. She loved her parents but rejected their religion and vegetarianism. She was close to her maternal grandparents who once accompanied their rabbi on a civil rights march with Martin Luther King. She hated her mother's insistence on tofu and platters of roasted vegetables, and adored her grandmother's homemade challah, sweet kugel, and oniony brisket.

Mr. Gillespie grew up in a conservative Lutheran family. The more he was forced to attend church, the greater he resisted religion and anything that reeked of preachiness. With each diploma...high school, college, and graduate school...the firmer he resisted any dogma. He was a quiet atheist who respected and advocated for anyone's personal beliefs, unless they involved handling snakes or sacrificial ceremonies.

Mr. and Mrs. Gillespie considered themselves best friends.

"Huggers like each other, but lovers hold hands," she said to her husband over dinner one night. She spoke gently, the way she tended to her roses, and he listened with tender, understanding eyes. "We're huggers, not hand holders."

A few months after divorcing, Mr. Gillespie bought the small bungalow next door to his former wife's. He immediately repainted it in subdued grays and browns, further distinguishing between their individual styles. She kept his name and his enduring friendship. They both lived contentedly as unmarried next-door neighbors. Sundays were suppers at each other's homes, even-dates at hers and odds at his. She cooked what she called serious foods. Meals that took time to develop flavors and demonstrated purpose: stews, chowders, quiches, roasts. She called Mr. Gillespie's meals happy foods. Easy-to-make, no recipe necessary, convenient, uncomplicated: steaks, scallops, salads, anything out of a container, and any prepared food picked up at the neighborhood market.

Those dinners were spent sharing news of the week and, because both were teachers, professional anecdotes. Mrs. Gillespie taught at the local elementary school, and Mr. Gillespie was the history department chair at the community college. Over the years, they had both lost some of their initial idealism, grew some cynicism, lamented the distraction of most technology, but remained positive about the impact they had on the lives of their students. Most of their dinnertime was spent talking about work.

"The principal told me that I've used up my budget for pencil sharpeners," said Mrs. Gillespie.

"You have a pencil sharpener budget?"

"It seems that I do. I also have overzealous children who love sharpening crayons instead of their fat pencils. So far I'm on my fourth pencil sharpener and the year is barely halfway over."

"Some parents are suggesting pencils are archaic instruments and too much time is spent learning how to hold them to form letters. They say, 'printing and handwriting are going the way of the abacus, slide rules, and needing to learn multiplication tables.' It's an oral world of voice commands and time for more creative thinking. They say I should be using tablets and other technology to teach the alphabet."

"They'll sing another tune when batteries are no longer available."

"Others question any electronics and want more blocks and creative play. I think the world is more divided at even the elementary level."

Mr. Gillespie summarized, "Those who want more blocks will hoard and hide batteries to frustrate the artificial intelligentsia. There will be a civil war between the Montessori and tech institute graduates. The middle class of reasonable utilitarianism is disappearing like their economy. There will be no happiness left, just remorse and bewilderment."

"Oh, dear, are we becoming too cynical?"

"We resist. We are teachers."

Mrs. Gillespie rarely watched television and the newspaper would not carry the story of the murder till the morning after the tragedy. Mr. Gillespie was waiting on his porch for Mrs. Gillespie to arrive home from Saturday errands. He ran to her driveway and waited for her to get out of her car before wrapping his arms around her. She looked up wide-eyed and with a confused expression. He pulled her close and told her the horrible news. He felt her slump in his arms before she straightened and wept into his shoulder.

"Her brother Seth is one of my pupils," she sobbed into Mr. Gillespie's shoulder. "How could this happen."

"You know that Wink is a colleague. I can't believe what has happened."

They sat on her front porch and he provided the few details that had emerged from neighbor's and colleague's frantic phone calls. From what he could gather, her mother Pinky was sitting on their front porch with their dogs Flora and Fauna while Rose was playing on the lawn. Apparently, she was killed instantly from a gun fired from some unknown location. The police are investigating. It was a bullet out of nowhere, with no sound, no warning, no explanation."

Monday morning arrived like a curtain of sadness, as though the universe had blanketed a bad mood over the entire town. Mrs. Gillespie had no idea how to address Seth's absence from class. Fortunately, her other students had no idea Seth's younger sister had been killed over the weekend. She thought that other parents must have been keeping the news from their youngsters and so they treated the day like any other. They came prepared to build block structures, learn letters, have big books read to them, and engage in the social development encouraged in kindergarten: how to share, say please and thank you, and get along with simple courtesies. They were expected to learn how to do school, not to cope with the evilness of the real world. Mrs. Gillespie worried over Seth's eventual attendance. Would he be gone a week while his family sat shiva? She wasn't sure that Seth's family even practiced the ritual. How should she welcome Seth back? How does one deal with death at such a young age?

At lunch she asked other teachers for their advice. She heard the predictable advice: Listen, listen, listen. Meet him where he is? Don't say everything is going to be alright? Let him be alone if he needs to be alone. If he needs a hug, give a hug. Don't try to explain death. Allow him to own his own feelings. Mrs. Gillespie understood the listening advice; nothing else made any sense. She decided that waiting for Seth to come back to school was the worst thing she could do.

She made a vegetarian lasagna and a large, tossed salad and was at Wink's and Pinky's front door the next day after school was out. Dressed in a plain black dress with a torn black ribbon pinned to the left shoulder, she stepped up onto the porch, the same porch from where Pinky watched her daughter Rose playing with glee and collapse into eternity, and noticed the door was slightly ajar, an invitation for mourners to enter without knocking. Mrs. Gillespie was now certain that Wink and Pinky must be sitting shiva. She recalled the first time she met Wink, a time long before he became a colleague of Mr. Gillespie's. She was flooded with the memory of Wink at Seymour S. Seymour's funeral. She had taught two of Mr. Seymour's grandchildren and remembered Mr. Seymour telling her of his young friend, a boy with six fingers, with whom he frequently took walks. "He's a special boy with special talents." She went out of her way to introduce herself to then twelve-year-old Wink and mention how much Mr. Seymour valued their friendship.

Now, memories emerged like long-lost, unopened packages sitting in the corner of an attic waiting to be found after too many dusty years. Mr. Seymour had described Wink as a boy gifted with the skill to absorb wisdom as his own without subsequent pretentiousness or arrogance. "He always amazes me with his ability to listen, to listen with genuine openness. It's been a privilege to have such a young friend at the end of my life." She remembered that Mr. Seymour had lost an infant grandchild during the time she was teaching one of his grandchildren, and how his endearing kindness to his living grandchildren was present every time he and his wife came to school events. "We give them love with no expectations. Some call that unconditional love. We're not so technical."

Mrs. Gillespie paused before pushing open the front door with feelings of reassurance from the memory of Mr. Seymour and dread over the situation at hand. Her intention had been to stop in, deliver a meal, offer respects to Wink and Pinky, and spend a bit of time with Seth. She entered and noticed the others milling about, dressed in subdued clothes, talking in low voices, appearing like shadows who had a place to be with despairing purpose. The room felt like a void of emptiness. A young life had been struck down, and with it, a spirit had been torn from everyone attending shiva, from the universe. Wink and Pinky sat in straight-backed chairs holding hands. Mrs. Gillespie would take away the image of Wink's six-fingered left hand tenderly holding Pinky's right hand on his knee. The entire time she was in that somber room, Wink and Pinky never let go of one another.

A person unknown to Mrs. Gillespie thanked her for coming and directed her to leave the food in the kitchen, which she did before intending to offer her condolences to Wink and Pinky. But before she could make her way over to them, Seth appeared from behind the kitchen island and grabbed ahold of Mrs. Gillespie's purse, which was dangling from the crook of her left arm.

"Mrs. G, you came," said Seth with what he had been taught to be his inside voice.

Mrs. Gillespie looked at Seth who was dressed in a stiff white Oxford shirt and black Levi's, but barefoot, which seemed oddly appropriate. He also had a torn black ribbon pinned to his shirt pocket. Mrs. Gillespie wondered if he had any notion of what that meant. He looked up with hazel eyes not yet old enough to contain accumulated sadness. They were full of questions and confusion. She bent over and whispered, "I came to see you."

Seth pulled Mrs. Gillespie toward the kitchen door leading to an outside deck. Once outside, he grabbed her hand and quietly said, "My sister Rose died. I don't know why."

Mrs. Gillespie wrapped both of her hands around Seth's, like holding a fragile kitten. She continued holding his hand as she sat on a deck chair bringing her face parallel to Seth's. She had never dealt with the death of one of her student's siblings. Most often, loss for one of her students came from a friend moving away, a pet dying or the death of a grandparent, aunt or uncle, but never a parent or sibling. She felt fortunate that those situations were best handled by her student's parents, and simply reported to her during daily classroom show and tell time. This was different. Rather than waiting for Seth's return to school, she had chosen to enter his space, coming to his home. There was no show and tell. There were no facts to be shared. There was his question of why.

She continued holding his hand. Tears clouded her eyes. She waited, listening.

8

Stanley

I never understood my grandfather Seymour till the end of his life, when I was well into my thirties. I thought of him as an odd bird who wore an attention-getting red beret and red tennis shows and frequently spouted words I had difficulty perceiving. "Someday you'll understand. On that day, you'll understand there is really no understanding, just acceptance." Huh? Was this advice or word salad coming from a crazy old kook. I was still in the throes of developing empathy, a process that continues.

He and my grandmother were well into early retirement when I was born. The memories of my grandmother all involve food. She seemed to always be standing in front of a vintage O'Keefe and Merritt stove stirring something that I looked forward to eating. The aromas from her kitchen were often a mix of oatmeal cookies and chicken soup. At least, that's what I remember: Grandma wearing a well-stained apron, fluffy pink slippers, with her curly blue hair in rollers and a babushka while cooking and Seymour sitting in the living room reading his newspapers from front to back pages, morning and evening editions.

Grandpa insisted that I call him by his first name, even though it was the same as his middle and last. He said he was too young to be call Grandpa. I understood that he worked in some profession that required college degrees but didn't realize how educated he was until after he had passed and his personal history was revealed through eulogies. My entire family history was more of a mystery than an open book. It's probably the reason I became a history teacher; a twist of knowing little about one's own past yet driven to study the pasts of others.

Those funeral stories revealed that Grandpa Seymour was an advocate. He had a law degree but didn't practice law. Apparently he earned a substantial living being an advocate for other people's causes. Grandpa...I insisted on calling him Grandpa near the end of his life, which he said was fine now that he was old...never spoke of himself. There was no personal advocacy. I remember him once telling me that it was important to "stand for something with passion and commitment."

He talked a lot about others, especially a six-fingered boy he had befriended. His name was Wink and I didn't know at the time that he would eventually have a profound effect on my life. Grandpa made a point of saying how special Wink was. They regularly took walks together, many times with Wink's mother, who had a dog-walking business. He insisted that I shake Wink's left hand whenever we should finally meet. I resisted, as I couldn't justify going out of my way to meet a boy many years my junior. We first met at Grandpa's funeral, when I noticed Wink who was wearing a red beret and red tennis shoes. At the time, I considered it a flagrant act of disrespect. After the service, Wink sought me out to offer his condolences. How does a kid know how to console? Was this what Grandpa thought so unique in this boy?

"Mr. Seymour was like a grandfather to me," said Wink with a mature presence I found off-putting at the time. "I am so sorry for your loss. I'm sure it leaves a huge hole in your heart."

I thought, what pre-teen talks like that?

Wink held out his right hand to shake mine, but I said, "My grandfather said we should shake left hands the first time." Reluctantly I held out my left and he grasped with his left and wiggled his extra finger in my palm. I jerked away and blurted, "Gross! Is this what my grandfather thought so special."

Wink kept a piercing gaze focused on my eyes, said nothing while remaining expressionless for what seemed like a torturous minute or two. Before he turned, and walked away he said, "Mr. Seymour told me just before he died that in the end all we have are the histories we've lived."

I felt foolish and thought I had violated some secret code. What did Wink know of history, personal or otherwise? The irony was that we both became history professors at the same college, where I had been teaching for over twenty years when Wink first began. I made a point of seeking him out at the faculty orientation. I hadn't seen him since Grandpa's funeral, and I still carried the shame of my reaction to his left-handed handshake.

"Wink, I'd like to shake your hand again; this time with an apology for my previous insensitivity and respect for your accomplishment and the honor of beginning a collegial relationship."

He held out his left hand and smiled with a warning that there'd be a wiggle. "Mr. Seymour said that histories can change if both parties are willing."

We shook, he wiggled his extra finger, and I sensed a bit of the endearing humor Grandpa must have experienced whenever he was with Wink.

We didn't become friends, probably due to our age difference. No doubt the generational gap influenced the relationships we kept. I was also the type of teacher who kept his head down, minded my own business, and chose to avoid expressing an opinion. Wink was a more engaging presence. Students signed up for his classes before rounding out their schedules with the rest of us. There was no jealousy toward Wink's charisma. We had similar charm when we were young professors. His energy helped to invigorate a department that had been in decline as the business and computer sciences divisions grew. Sometimes it takes personality to overcome the economics of choice.

The day I learned of the tragedy that befell Wink and his wife Pinky changed everything. I could not believe an anonymous bullet had struck down their two-year-old daughter Rosie. The horror of shootings, mass murders, and growing violence had become normal daily news. I quickly learned the victims' and perpetrators' names. I could make sense of those senseless acts. But I could not reconcile a bullet coming out of nowhere. I had been teaching a class "The History of Violence in Modern America" for several years, although interest had been waning with the ever-growing rise in shootings.

Shortly after Rose's funeral, I felt compelled to do something. I had never been a do something sort of person. I was an observer, mostly by reading books, periodicals, and watching the news. I led a stagnant life, a life of comfort with a stable wife and two grown kids who we managed to raise and find their way out of the house without much drama.

I made a sandwich board out of two pieces of heavy cardboard. On one side I painted a bright red happy face, on the other a Kelly-green peace sign. Above each drawing I printed in heavy, black letters "**SHOOT ME FIRST.**" Much later, after I had acted, I was asked why the happy face and peace sign.

"I've always believed peace was a funny thing. It usually takes a war to arrive at peace, and vice versa."

My wife came into the garage and saw what I was doing. She stood the way only a wife can stand when disbelief encounters reality: head cocked open-mouthed, scrunched eyes where a crease appears between the brows, with one hand on a hip and the other waving unintentionally.

"Stanley Seymour." Always Stanley Seymour when there was concern. "What are you doing?"

"Grandpa Seymour once told me to stand for something. I've finally figured out what he meant. It's time."

"Where might you be making this stand?"

"Downtown in the middle of the roundabout."

"Stanley, I'm worried you won't be standing for long."

"That might be the point."

She shook her head and said she was going inside to call our son and daughter and report that I've lost my mind. She was certainly the whimsical side of my sandwich board. Once the kids got involved, there would probably be hostilities.

Yes, I acted. I drove downtown and stood on a grassy knoll in the middle of a roundabout wearing my sandwich board. It was a warm day and I wore blue board shorts, a white sleeveless cotton shirt, and a broad brimmed straw hat. I paid attention to keeping my spine straight and my shoulders relaxed, as I intended to stand as long as possible. I wasn't sure if I should stand still like the Statue of Liberty holding a lamp to show the way, not knowing which way to go. Or perhaps I should rotate like a Calder kinesthetic mobile, after all I was in the midst of a traffic circle. I decided to stand still, like a stoic making a statement with a simple sign and no suggestive gestures.

For the first thirty minutes or so, nothing happened. I tried to take note of the vehicles as they passed by. Drivers did not seem to take notice, probably because negotiating traffic circles is new for most Americans. They're busy trying to figure out what exit to take them out of their circular entrapment. Then I began to see cars making their second run through the circle, and some went around more than once with a honk or a wave. I couldn't tell if it was a supportive or negative gesture. At one point, a driver stopped, rolled down his window, and shouted, "You go, fool! You just might be the first!" I responded with a tight smile and a nod. He drove off after showing me a poorly manicured middle finger.

The dome-shaped hill I stood on was covered in coarse grass and an abundance of dandelions. I thought of my own lawn and the hours I spent pulling dandelions while trying to make my lawn the most pristine in the neighborhood. What was the point? A neighbor always chastised me for my dandelion eradication, telling me how important they were to the environment as pollinators and a healthy food source. Lost in reverie, I began a slow rotation, no longer hearing honks, shouts, or fingers. Suddenly, the sprinklers came on and woke me from my trance. A group of adolescent boys stood across the street on the sidewalk laughing and shouting, "Be the first old man." I stood still once again, becoming drenched and smiled back at them with wordless resolve while my cardboard sandwich began to blister from water and sun.

The next afternoon, with a dried and damaged sandwich board, I returned to my station. I was surprised to find an older woman standing on the knoll. She wore a black linen dress, bright red lipstick, and a white smock covered with fingerpaint smeared above the hem and "**SHOOT ME FIRST**" printed across the bib.

"I'm Mrs. Gillespie and I heard about you. You work with Mr. Gillespie. I'm a kindergarten teacher for Wink's and Pinky's oldest son. I know who you are and I knew your grandfather. I admired his individual style, his thoughtfulness, and his flair for red accents. He'd be proud of you. I'm here to stand with." She paused and looked up at my bushy, brown hair before adding, "You should be wearing a red beret."

"I appreciate your commitment," and those were the only words we uttered for the next two hours. She and I both understood that silent protest was much more effective than chants and fist-wagging. It was easy to tolerate the frequent taunts with grace and solemnity with a partner who shared a common message.

My second surprise that afternoon was when my wife arrived with a bottle of water and a tuna sandwich. "Stanley, you need to stay hydrated and eat something," and, noticing Mrs. Gillespie, she added, "I'm sorry. I didn't know there were two of you."

"I'm fine. He had no idea I'd be here." Mrs. Gillespie explained who she was. My wife gave her a hug, which was really out of character, and said she'd be back with more water and another sandwich.

"She's a lovely lady, Stanley."

"Please, call me Stan." And we continued our silent watch.

On the third day, the threatening gestures began to be outnumbered by shouts of encouragement. A few newcomers joined us and asked how they could help. I thanked them for coming and asked them to stand quietly. It was also the day when a group of seven or eight men marched up the sidewalk, dressed in camo and shouldering assault-style weapons. They took up a position with glaring looks and ramrod postures, apparently trying to intimidate us. They kept their guns slung over their shoulders, fortunately never pointing them at us. They, too, had their silent message. Shortly after they arrived, two police cars pulled into the traffic circle, exited on the street where the riflemen stood, and parked their black and whites. Four officers, three men and one woman, approached the riflemen and spoke to them before the woman officer crossed to our spot on the knoll. I recognized her as Officer Jen, one of my neighbors who lived at the other end of my long block with her husband and two young children. We didn't socialize and were more of the how's-it-going-in-passing type of neighbors.

"How's it going, Stan?"

"Okay, I guess."

"You wouldn't happen to have a permit for this gathering?" asked Officer Jen.

"I didn't think about that. Do I really need one?"

"Not yet. If your group numbers more than twenty, you will."

"It's not my group. I'm here on my own and have no control over what others are doing."

"That may be true," said Officer Jen in her even, non-confrontive voice. "However, you do need to know the rules." She turned and walked away, nodding at the other three officers before they entered their cars, took time to make some notes, and drove off.

Mrs. Gillespie told our new supporters that if they returned she would have smocks for them. They asked how else they could help. She responded by giving her address and asking them to drop by her home later that night to help prepare the smocks. I never heard of anyone who kept a supply of plain white smocks. Then, again, I couldn't say I was acquainted with any other kindergarten teachers. I assumed she must have bought them at a closeout sale. I did know that elementary teachers were skilled at finding bargains.

On the fourth day, Mrs. Gillespie returned with more than a dozen other supporters all wearing smocks, showing creases from having been taken fresh from a box, with "**SHOOT ME FIRST**" printed across their bibs. We did not yet number more than twenty, but the group of gunslingers across the street were now far above that number. I didn't notice any rule enforcers in the vicinity.

My wife came by with two coolers. One was filled with bottles of water, juices, and sodas, the other with a variety of sandwiches and bags of chips and cookies. She placed them at the foot of the grassy knoll, announced that no voice should be silenced because of hunger, and then drove off. I think she may have begun to think of me as a little less crazy.

On the fifth day, we continued our silent vigil. Mrs. Gillespie passed out another box of painted smocks to some newcomers. I think there were a dozen smocks to a box, so now we were definitely in need of a permit. The mob of pro-whatever-they-were-for had also grown larger. Yet, there was mysteriously no police presence. Was the official in charge of protest groups on vacation or was this a case of blind neglect? We did have grandmotherly Mrs. Gillespie on our side and maybe that was a deterrent to enforcement. She really stood out in our small, smock-clad group who appeared to be insane enough to die for a cause. I remembered that there was a poet or a statesman who once said he would not kill for his country, but he would die for it. I don't think I was prepared to die for anything other than a young child killed by an anonymous bullet.

I was the only one without a smock. I preferred my slowly disintegrating sandwich board, which had yet to endure another soaking. In fact, the sprinklers had not come on a second time. Perhaps a city worker disabled the sprinklers in support. The lawn was showing signs of wear and tear, but it was hard to abuse a weedy knoll anyway. I took stock of the those who had joined together to take a stand. Other than Mrs. Gillespie, I had not been introduced to any of them. I don't believe they had introduced themselves to one another. They did adopt a nickname. They called themselves the "Smockers." As I walked among the Smockers, I felt a sense of peace just before an echoing crack of ear-piercing sound that brought all of us to our knees. Someone had discharged a rifle, not aimed at us but into the sky. I immediately regained my footing as the Smockers did, too. We blankly faced the crowd of gun lovers who were scrambling to tackle whoever had either intentionally or accidentally fired their rifle. Four police cruisers quickly emerged from each street leading into the traffic circle, sirens blaring. They must have been parked out of sight while we tended to our demonstrations. Before any of the officers exited their vehicles, Mrs. Gillespie scurried across that street like a squirrel with a purpose.

"Who do you fools think you are?" she shouted. "You shoot into the air without thinking of the consequences. Was it one of you who killed Rose?"

The crowd of NRA sympathizers froze as Mrs. Gillespie, half the size of nearly all the gun-toters, raced toward them shaking her index finger at them with a voice meant for playground duty.

"He is the one you want, lady!" exclaimed a tall, bearded man. "He shot his gun without authorization. He's the one you want."

Two police officers surrounded the identified shooter, confiscated his rifle, and pulled him off to the side. Mrs. Gillespie stood, feet firmly planted, continuing to wag a finger, and emphatically replied, "He's merely the symptom. You are all the disease. Don't blame your ugliness on one wart. A child died because someone discharged a bullet into the air. Probably having fun without knowing the consequences."

I remained standing with my feet firmly in place. Mrs. Gillespie was the only one who left the knoll, finding her voice, and making clear her passion. The other Smockers began continuously chanting, "Shoot me first."

The camo-clad mob appeared to recoil, not sure what to make

of those willing to sacrifice themselves without harming others. I stood with my aging sandwich board, silent but feeling the electricity of chanting voices recharging my inner resolve. Grandpa Seymour must be smiling in heaven.

9

Seth

The world finally made sense when Seth learned the binary number system. Before then, his young life had been tragically altered when his younger sister Rose had been shot dead by an anonymous bullet. His life seemed to unravel like a ball of yarn being pawed at by an aggressive house cat. Seth was a serious child who was not mature enough to comprehend permanent loss. He was in kindergarten at the time and he came to cherish his kindergarten teacher's kindness. At his sister's funeral, Mrs. Gillespie quietly held his hand and from that moment became the singular adult who would forever influence his life.

When his class was learning numbers, Mrs. Gillespie observed Seth's mathematical precociousness. Seth had the early ability to find patterns in random shapes and especially in numbers. He was Mrs Gillespie's only kindergartener who learned the Base 10 numeral system through self-discovery while playing with number blocks and writing down the values formed by those colorful pieces. With little guidance, he learned midway through kindergarten how to add and subtract. He lost himself in numbers. It became a distraction, his therapy, for dealing with his sister's loss. Mrs. Gillespie once told him that mathematics would help him find meaning in an often-chaotic world. What she didn't know was that Seth's gift would also be his greatest flaw: his inability to appreciate nuance and an off-putting sense of righteousness, which would eventually lead to one particular episode of outrageousness.

Seth learned to count before he spoke in sentences. He fondly remembered sitting on his father's lap touching each of the five fingers on his father's right hand and the six on the left. With his father's assistance he quickly learned a chant while touching each finger, "pinky one, ring two, index three, pointer four, thumb five," before moving to the left hand, "thumb six, pointer seven, index eight, bonus index nine, ring ten, pinky eleven."

Wink often told his son, "Counting is the beginning of learning to count as a person. Know your numbers and you'll amount to anything you'll want to be." Seth learned by his mid-teens, his father's proclivity for attempts at profundity stemmed from a childhood relationship with Mr. Seymour, an elderly gentleman Wink often described as a "second grandfather with exceptional wisdom." As Seth began to individuate from his family, he dismissed his father's attempts at Mr. Seymour-like insights as silly and a waste of time.

Seth progressed in school, skipping second grade and being offered special math instruction as a gifted and talented student. He found learning Base Two an extraordinary experience. He came to believe that everything could be controlled with just two digits: zero and one. The notion of a binary system astounded him. He saw the world as a product of on and off switches, blacks and whites, good and evil, right and wrong, yes and no, either/or, and permission and denial. There were no gray areas for Seth, only absolutes. There were clear, unarguable answers to every big question or concrete answers not yet discovered.

Seth found solace in numbers. He glided through elementary, middle, and high school doing well enough in what he referred to as "impractical classes" like English, history, and art, and excelling in anything involving numbers…math, chemistry, economics. He majored in mathematics in college, earned a master's degree in statistics, but failed to complete a PhD program because his advising professor said he lacked imagination. "You are an outstanding arithmetician but not a mathematician," he said when advising Seth to pursue a career in statistics. "You might find baseball sabermetrics interesting. Empirical work would be much more your strength than theoretical."

The good news was that Seth loved baseball. He and his father spent many summer days at the local park watching amateur games, whether Little League, high school or adult leagues. He easily learned to keep score while in his early school days. His collections of scorecards were kept in binders labeled by year and went back for decades. They were catalogued in chronological order with special games tagged with slips of Post-it Note paper protruding like road signs, dated and notated with words such as "no-hitter" or "future big leaguer". Mixed in were professional games, with only purple tags distinguished the pros from all others. Becoming a baseball sabermetrics expert was the perfect career choice. He sold his services as a freelancer to college and professional baseball teams. He earned a very comfortable living using statistics to provide evidence-based advice.

Seth had no problem using his view of correctness to justify intervention. His early binary worldview coupled with an innate ability to manipulate situations compelled him to intervene whenever he thought something was unfair. It might have been confronting another kindergartener who hogged the blocks or stayed too long at the painting station, or when he reported to his sixth-grade teacher that some classmates had cheated on a test. He was smart enough to keep his identity secret and not suffer the wrath of angry schoolmates. He was like a double agent working both sides of the truth, both an adult's and child's version.

Seth grew to be a tall man with narrow hips and shoulders and a protruding belly. His brown hair was cut short military-style every two weeks. He smelled of the sandalwood shaving soap he used every morning. He took his grooming seriously. He dressed in dark suits with open-neck white dress shirts and black Oxford shoes, which were shined with each haircut by Oscar. Oscar was the seventy-something shoe shiner who had worked at the one-and-only barber shop in town that still featured barbers who still offered a shave and honed their razors on a leather strop.

Seth was rarely noticed when entering a crowded room; yet he noticed and quickly labeled everyone: nice guy, a girl with the potential to be pretty, a clique with a meanness about them. His wife Jenny was quick to agree. They met in grad school, where she, too, was a mathematics major whose career goal was to earn a master's degree and teach at a community college. Being a tall woman with little to say was what Seth first noticed. Their romance developed along with the solution of advanced calculus problems and an infatuation with graphical representations.

Jenny thought Seth was a genius with social limitations but didn't care. She appreciated the confidences he shared with her and believed his labeling was merely sarcasm, which she found humorous and endearing. When her mother questioned if Seth was the right man to marry, she answered by saying he came from good family stock and that numbers didn't lie.

"A lifetime commitment isn't about theorems and axioms. There are intangibles like love, affection and empathy."

"Mom, we both love the security of givens. Besides, he's cute in an Ichabod Crane kind of way."

On weekends, when there wasn't an important baseball game to watch, they both lounged about their tidy home wearing matching T-shirts with "Life is Good" printed boldly across the front. And life was good until Seth began noticing a disturbing trend in their town.

Tents, make-shift tents, cardboard shanties, and unwashed people began occupying public spaces along with a variety of untamed and hungry-looking dogs. Litter began piling and human waste stunk behind bushes on the periphery of manicured park lawns. Seth had read of the homeless issues in larger, urban areas and was shocked that it was happening in his idyllic town. He believed that some of the homeless were a result of mental illness or downright bad luck. He also believed that many of the younger homeless were simply a growing group of entitled children who embraced anarchy and the belief that their home was wherever they chose to drop their backpacks and pitch tents. They didn't identify as homeless, rather calling themselves houseless, as though there was something noble and more meaningful with the shift of terminology. He believed the true homeless population had something taken away through loss or unexpected circumstance and not by their own choosing. He also believed that self-identifying "houseless" were simply sponging off the generosity of others. One was right and the other wrong.

"Jenn, we should so something to help the genuine homeless. But the others are selfish vagrants who take without contributing. They are a scourge and need to be told to get a job or get out of our town, just like what a good parent does when their able-bodied children need to grow up and move out of the house."

"What should we do, Seth?"

Seth had no answer. He was confused by his own certainty.

His abhorrence began with street beggars, although a counselor might have told him it began when his sister Rose was killed and resulted in unresolved anger. Seth didn't believe in psychology. He thought of it as a soft science, not something provable like statistics. He could not fathom why any able-bodied person could possibly stand by the entrance of a market with a sign asking for spare change, much less ask, "My car ran out of gas, can you help." He was convinced nobody's car had run dry or whether or not those he called bums even owned a vehicle. At first, he would look away and continue walking. But one day, walking with his parents and his wife Jenny, he looked directly into an obese and heavily tattooed woman and snapped, "Get a job and have some personal pride." Jenny softly told Seth he should be more compassionate. His parents picked up their pace, putting some distance between themselves and their son. After Seth and Jenny caught up, Wink turned to his son and reminded him that difference was not always a choice.

Later, Seth's mother Pinky asked him what his outrage at that woman was all about.

"Most of those people are able to work. I think they are making choices that we are paying for. It's not right."

Adding to his own frustration were the actions of his parents. Pinky volunteered two days a week at a free meals feeding station located in the city's largest park. A local group calling themselves Advocates for Decency prepared hot meals, which were served every afternoon to anyone who showed up. Wink helped with park clean-up every Saturday. The Advocates for Decency regularly attended city council meetings calling for Port-a-Potties and washing stations to be set up in the park and at other locations about town where, as Seth began referring to them, the "unkempt and spongers" frequently gathered. A subgroup of Advocates collected used clothing, which they distributed via a community closet located in the town's library. Additionally, they approached those who appeared to be the neediest with offers to do their laundry.

"Mom and dad, how can you possibly justify what you are doing. It's like giving out engraved invitations to stick around. You are contributing to the problem. Can't you see what's happening?"

"It's about empathy and care, Seth, not about being judgmental," said Pinky with a soft touch on her son's forearm.

Wink added, "I wonder what Mr. Seymour might have thought. I'm guessing he would have said it's complicated and that sometimes the answer comes through actions, whatever they might be."

"That makes absolutely no sense, dad," said Seth as he walked away, shoulders slumped, and shaking his head before turning back and adding, "Have you smelled the shit and piss from the former flower beds in the park? There's no excuse or acceptance of that. Mr. Seymour would have been appalled."

Seth began having sleepless nights as he perseverated over what he felt was a falling apart society. He likened his town's and the entire country's predicament as a precursor to the fall of the Roman Empire.

"Our entire culture is about to go over a precipice, dragging all of us into a dark abyss."

Jenny sipped at her iced tea while they sat on their patio. It was a hot day. She wore a yellow "Life is Good" T-shirt, tan shorts, open-toed sandals, and smelled of lavender soap while listening to Seth. Her attention calmed Seth.

"It's a very sad situation. What can we do? I'm feeling as lost as you."

Seth recalled the time Wink told him the story of when Stanley and Mrs. Gillespie protested gun violence. It had become known as the SHOOT ME FIRST standoff. He remembered Mrs. Gillespie in similar ways that Wink remembered Mr. Seymour. Mrs. Gillespie was an important adult influence in Seth's life, just as Mr. Seymour continued to be in his father's.

Even with their passing, they remained present like advice books or articles checked out from a library or downloaded from a website. This was a time when Seth wished to talk with Mrs. Gillespie. He loved his parents, but they were too instructive. Jenny was a wonderful listener but didn't give advice, which Seth appreciated. Mrs. Gillespie listened, synthesized, and asked probing questions which helped him to think. She was the only person in his life who could prod him to consider alternatives to right and wrong and move him away from his binary thinking. But she wasn't there anymore and he felt as bewildered as a lost hiker without a compass.

He and Jenny decided to take a walk. He needed exercise to try and ease the tension he felt building inside. In addition to his difficulty sleeping, he had recently begun to hyperventilate. He paid a visit to the hospital's emergency room thinking he might be having a heart attack. The doctor quickly diagnosed the breathing issue as anxiety and recommended a breathing exercise and also some choices of medication. Seth said no to medication and found that breathing into a paper bag worked well. Unfortunately, he didn't have a bag with him on the walk and he was beginning to experience short, rapid breathing signaling the onset of a panic attack.

Jenny noticed Seth's difficulty with catching his breath and pasty complexion and asked if he needed to find a place to sit. They found a bench at a bus stop where Seth lowered his head between his knees while Jenny massaged the back of his neck. She could feel a cool dampness but didn't ask again if Seth was okay. She knew he was too proud to admit to any failings on his part. After about fifteen minutes, he sat up and proclaimed himself ready to resume walking. Just as they approached the corner, Seth and Jenny were stopped by one of the homeless, a young man in his late teens or early twenties, reeking of cigarette smoke, long blond hair beginning to form dreadlocks, unshaven, wearing threadbare denim pants, a hoodie, and an orange "Life is Good" T-shirt. In his left hand he held a newer smartphone. held out his right hand and asked for spare change. Seth noticed a small group of his compatriots waiting for him on the sidewalk across the street.

One shouted, "C'mon dude, they're not going to give you anything! Let's get to the park."

Seth's anxiety changed to anger. The "Life is Good" T-shirt felt like a profane taunt. His pale face turned red and he felt his back stiffen. He moved closer to the boy as Jenny backed away. This was a question of right or wrong. Act or don't act. Fix it or ignore it. Seth thought of a simple binary solution.

"Seth let's go. Leave him alone."

"Just a word with this needy, offensive young man," said Seth with a surprisingly measured tone. He placed his hand on the boy's lower back and moved him aside while lowering his voice like a co-conspirator and asked, "Does your phone work?"

"No, it's turned off. I need to charge it. There's an outlet over at the park." Being socially clueless and not capable of reading body language, the boy thought that Seth was about to help out after all.

"Oh, good, I wouldn't want you to record what I'm about to tell you."

"Cool, I get it."

"No, I don't think you do. I don't think you get it at all. Here's the deal and listen carefully because I won't repeat what I'm about to say and I'll just deny it if you try to tell anyone. You have no credibility around here. So, here's the deal: I have a gun and I'm going to use it if you and your friends don't leave this town before it gets dark tonight. I will come and I will shoot you. I won't hesitate. You can go somewhere else and ruin their town, but not here. Not here anymore. Do you understand?" Seth projected a steeliness in his eyes as he looked down at a now frightened boy. "I'm deadly serious."

Seth and Jenny walked home. When Jenny asked what Seth had said to the boy, Seth said he strongly suggested that the boy and his friends move on to another town as soon as possible. Seth didn't keep secrets from Jenny, but he didn't reveal the details of his strongly-stated encouragement. He didn't own a gun, never intended to own one, and believed guns were statistically a curse on humanity. Later that night he found the need for a brown paper bag and a wish that he could talk to Mrs. Gillespie again. If only to ask for forgiveness.

10

Boyd

We could never have been so different. At least that's what Mrs. Gillespie said as we passed through her kindergarten class three years apart. My older brother Seth established expectations with his precocity for mathematics and his zealous right or wrong judgmental assessment of everything from who gets to use the paste pots and how many can be at the block station at any time. On the other hand, I was born laissez-faire. As the surviving twin after my sister Rose's murder, I became the happy-go-lucky kid who climbed a headstone at my sister's funeral and swung my legs back and forth while giggling. It was not humor I found. I was too young to understand that macabre events could be amusing. No, it was the simple joy of having climbed up on something as tall as me and feeling a two-year-old's sense of accomplishment; espoused as joyful noise despite the seriousness of the moment. Later and in a reflective moment, Mrs. Gillespie, who was present and holding Seth's hand during the solemn ceremony, excused it as the resilience that comes from a loving family. My parents expressed it as a two-year-old's sense of immediacy. I suppose they were both correct.

It was the beginning of my prankster days. When I grew old enough to know that socks were meant to be matched, I would sneak into my brother's room and rearrange his socks into mismatched pairs. Blacks with whites, stripes with argyles, anklet with calf-length. Seth generally ignored confronting me but was sure to report the infraction to mom and dad. They wrote it off as sibling rivalry and with a simple request to stop teasing Seth. There was the time I snuck into my third-grade classroom and placed a couple of frogs in my teacher's top desk drawer. I had captured the little green amphibians on the way to school, put them in my lunch pail along with my apple, grape juice box, and Swiss cheese sandwich. I was fortunate to be the first one to arrive at school. When Ms. Sullivan slid open the drawer to retrieve her roll book, the frogs leapt onto her lap. She barely flinched and calmly picked them up, excused herself for a moment, walked out the classroom door, and returned as though nothing had happened. She actually touched the frogs with a straight face, and perhaps a bit of a comical smirk. It was the first time I realized teachers were a special order of human beings. Mrs. Gillespie and Ms. Sullivan clearly fell into a category I thought of as belonging to a noble cabal with their own rules and rituals. They both carried themselves with poise, calm and an unshakeable quality which elevated them to godlike status. I was pretty sure Ms. Sullivan knew I was the culprit because, upon her return to the classroom, she managed a serious look with pleated brows and a close-lipped smile pointed in my direction. My classmates were frozen in disbelief as I smiled back at Ms. Sullivan. She never commented on the prank. She was also the first of several teachers I had crushes on.

My father had six fingers on his left hand. Perfectly formed and fully functional. He considered his rare condition, which some called a deformity, as a gift. I saw it as a gift of humor, an oddity, the quality of being different. Dad used to tell Seth and me that he learned from Mr. Seymour, who he called a second grandfather, that difference is what makes life valuable.

"Mr. Seymour told me to insist on shaking left hands so that I could give a little wiggle. He said it was like the gift of a diamond in the rough. Nobody desires a gem that looks like any other."

I wanted to be like my dad and spent hours trying to form a Hebrew National hotdog into an extra finger for my left hand. As hard as I tried as an eight-year-old, I lacked the manual dexterity to hold the kosher finger in place and give it the handshake wiggle just like dad when shaking left hands. I destroyed an entire package of hotdogs before my mother told me no more or it would come out of my feeble allowance. Fortunately, there were always a few pet dogs around to clean up hotdog debris.

Seth was a tall man with a rounded belly that gave him the illusion of slovenliness even though he was an impeccably groomed person. I was physically opposite, average height and lean, and dressed casually as opposed to his formality. His brown hair short, mine caramel-colored and shaggy. He smelled of sandalwood and I eschewed any perfumed products. I had a metabolism like my mother's and burned whatever calories I consumed. I was always hungry, always snacking with pretzels and jelly beans close at hand. Yet, we were close, bound together by family tragedy and our parents insistence that we love one another. I unconditionally supported him after his arrest. After all, he was always there for me through each of my breakups.

He called me a serial monogamist. It's true, I had many relationships lasting from a few dates to several months. I liked women of all shapes, sizes, colors, cultures, and economic status. I still do, although I have recently decided to seek out a Jewish girl. My mother is Jewish, which makes me Jewish even though I grew up without any religious education. When I was younger, my father said I was just sowing wild oats. As I grew older, he said I was not a very good farmer. Seth told me I didn't respect women. I told him I wasn't sure I respected myself. My lack of certainty did not sit well with my brother's righteous sense of certainty. He did like the idea of me narrowing the focus of my romantic pursuits to a Jewish girl.

"It's good to have a plan," he remarked the day after a five-month romantic entanglement ended with a lovely Southern belle whose political beliefs were completely unacceptable. "Maybe you should try a dating service. One for Jews. There's a logic to a matchmaker's methods. It'll be my treat."

I have yet to take him up on his generous offer, but I have begun to attend social events at the local synagogue. It's amazing how many older Jewish women are looking for a second or third husband with the assuredness of a confident real estate broker. The age difference between them and me is extreme, but intriguing. The women in my age group are very nervous and unsure of themselves. I have a theory that they gained their beauty in post-adolescence and lacked the experience of the high school dating scene. They had yet to experience the first blush of puppy love and were jumping into the dating pool like playful otters learning to swim for the first time. They huddled together around the punch bowl hoping for an eligible male to approach and ask for a dance. And there was a third group of men and women who were still unmatched and veterans of the temple get-togethers. They had developed a degree of nonchalance and appeared to be more interested in snacks and beverages rather than each other's company. I feared becoming a member of that group.

My brother's arrest put a damper on my pursuits. His wife Jenny called me one early evening while I was on a date with Keely, a dark-haired sabra visiting from Israel and looking for some companionship. I was actually feeling more deeply attracted to her than most first dates. She had a bright, toothy smile and a belly laugh that attracted unnecessary attention, but I didn't care because she laughed at all my silliness and that's all that mattered at the moment. Our meal at Zorba the Greek's Restaurant was interrupted when my cell phone cock-a-doodle-dooed.

"Seth has been arrested. We're at the downtown police station. Can you get down here right away. And please don't tell your parents."

"What happened."

"A huge misunderstanding. Please, get here as soon as you can."

That was the last I saw of Keely, which was too bad. I was just about to tell her the one Jewish joke I knew, but never got to it. A group of five Jewish women are eating lunch in a busy cafe. Nervously, their waiter approaches the table. 'Ladies,' he says. 'Is anything okay?'

Things were not apparently okay for my brother. Jenny was pacing in front of the police station. It was a cool, cloudless evening with a full moon reminding me of the interrogation lamp that I imagined Seth enduring after his arrest. I wasn't sure if Jenny's pacing was from worry or anger.

"Whatever you do, Boyd, be careful what you say to Wink and Pinky."

"Huh?"

"As brilliant as he is, I think he really screwed up."

"Huh?"

"Fortunately, he's being released without any charges."

"Huh?"

"A couple of the homeless falsely accused him of threatening to shoot them if they didn't leave town. The whole thing is ridiculous. What they put Seth through is an abomination. But I believe he really did threaten someone. He's been acting weird for several days ever since he confronted one while we were out walking. He won't talk to me about it."

"I still don't understand what's going on. Why am I here?"

"Seth wanted you to come down."

He emerged from the station wearing a "Life Was Good Before…" T-shirt, bold white block letters on black. He nodded at me, hugged Jenny, whispered something in her ear and asked if he and I could find a place to chat.

"Just the two of us, Boyd. Jenny is going to head home."

"What's with the shirt. I'm the funny brother, or did you forget?"

We were seated at the only all-night café in town, generally reserved for emergency technicians, hospital workers, night shift law enforcement, and those afflicted with sleep disorders seeking the comfort pie and a hot beverage.

"Have you noticed that the world is falling apart?"

"It's part of the natural life cycle, Seth. You're born and in a growth mode. You peak at a certain age. If you've been lucky enough to establish healthy habits and a certain level of financial security, you plateau for a few years before decay sets in. And then the next generation comes along. It's like the punch line to the only Jewish joke I know."

"Yeah, 'is anything okay?'"

"In your world it's a binary point-of-view, whether you are an optimist or a pessimist."

"Nothing in between?" asked Seth.

"You're looking for shadings?"

"I suppose I am."

I forked off a piece the lemon meringue pie I had ordered and took a sip of mint tea. It was a combination that always worked well for me. The mint complimented the lemon, although my brother said it should be the other way around. Seth sat with a glass of ice water and a bowl of vanilla ice cream topped with fresh strawberries. I reminded myself that the most unassuming café can sometimes have fairly good food.

Seth said, "You paint a mostly pessimistic view with your life cycle."

"Realistic. All things end. The sun will eventually burn out. Poof! There goes earth. It's a human conceit that we matter. All we try to do is extend mortality into immortality."

"How does trying to be a Jew fit with your existential beliefs?"

"Perfectly. We're Jews, Seth. It's in our nature to argue. And I'm not trying. It was inherited."

"Being a Jew is not biological," stressed Seth. "It's all invented."

"Yeah, I know. Still, it's a comforting notion. And I was just getting to know this sabra gal before Jenny called and interrupted what might have been a good time. What's going on, Seth?"

Seth reminded me about the time I pranked him when we were both in high school. He was always obsessed with cleanliness and personal hygiene. We shared a bedroom, a fairly large room, but shared, nonetheless. I never made my twin bed and often left dirty clothes on the floor. Seth's bed looked like something out of the Marine Corp handbook, drum tight and able to bounce a quarter off its surface. His side of the closet arranged like a department store display; mine with pants and shirts often hung askew. Our bathroom had two sinks and his sparkled under his daily care while mine was lucky if it was scoured once a month. One morning I dabbed some chunky peanut butter on the toilet seat waiting for Seth's outrage.

"Boyd!" he shouted. "What is this on the toilet seat?"

I slipped out of bed, faking a yawn, stretched and shuffled into the bathroom. I looked down at the toilet seat, swiped a bit of peanut butter with my index finger, tasted it, and casually replied, "Tastes like shit, Seth."

I laughed at Seth's memory. In that particular moment, I felt like I should have listened with more seriousness considering the circumstances.

My brother was trying to tell a story that somehow related to his current situation.

"And you've never even liked peanut butter. We didn't talk to one another for weeks. It just goes to show how some actions have unintended outcomes, no matter how unintentional those actions might be. What I mean is, I did something involving something I hate. You hate peanut butter and I hate guns."

"Are you seriously comparing the two?"

"Dumb analogy. You know I'm horrible with analogies. I think I'm trying to explain what happened."

"By comparing fake shit with guns?"

"No. By comparing one stupid act with another."

I finished my pie and asked for more hot water to refresh my tea while listening to Seth

tell me about his bad act. Mostly, he talked about his own guilt and shame, even though he legally got away with any wrong doing by virtue of quietly uttering his threat to a socially isolated and disreputable individual. When Seth finished confessing his actions, as though I was some sort of Catholic priest which really irked my secular Jewish sensibilities, I signaled to our server.

"I would love another piece of lemon meringue pie. My brother would like a large slice of humble pie or its equivalent."

For the first time, I took note of our server, an immense woman wearing a stereotypical waitress uniform, black dress, white apron, and clunky black Dr. Scholl shoes. She efficiently managed the entire restaurant, diners coming and going, sitting or ordering takeout. Despite her size, she moved with a ballerina's grace. Her head was attached to her neck without definition, all one piece like a walrus's, a large cone that swiveled keeping an eye on all her charges. She was the most unusual looking woman I had ever seen and I had to keep myself from rudely staring.

She replied like a skilled improvisor, "Humble pie used to be a specialty, but now we serve the humblest of pies. How does apple or peanut butter sound?"

I choked back a guffaw over the peanut butter reference and, although Seth objected, ordered him a piece of apple pie ala mode.

"Here's the deal, Seth. You screwed up and need to own it. You know better than anyone the difference between right and wrong. Unless you tell Jenny and mom and dad the truth, you'll be haunted by your foolishness."

I could not recall a time I had ever seen Seth cry. Yet, tears began to well in the corners of his dark eyes. Our food was set before us and the walrus noticed my brother's shifting emotional state. I don't believe in karma or whether coincidence has any special meeting, but what she did next made we wonder. She placed an oversized hand on Seth's shoulder and gave him a squeeze. And then she repeated her own edited version of a famous Beatles lyric: I am she as you are he as you are me/And we are all together/See how they run like pigs from a gun/See how they fly/I'm crying.

The guffaw that I managed to squelch over the peanut butter reference mysteriously transferred to Seth and came out loud and with a copious amount of spittle. I wondered if I had also mysteriously communicated my walrus imagery. Our good-natured server smiled down at Seth, fortunately without tusks, and said, "You've got it. Goo goo g'joob, goo goo goo g'joob."

Reunion

6:00 a.m.

Mel and Sylvie had been taking morning walks ever since Mel's retirement as a stone mason. It had been almost twenty years, now. Up every day, rain or shine, with their fifth black standard poodle, each one named Rex regardless of its gender. This Rex happened to be a female with all four legs, unlike the first Rex, a tripod, and the third Rex, another tripod. What distinguished this Rex from all other Rexes was a white blaze on her muzzle below her mouth. It gave Rex the look of a library scholar who quietly knew and understood the world's wisdom. Mel and Sylvie always liked the idea of dogs with a difference because of their son Wink, who had six fingers on his left hand, making him unique. And Wink had been raised to appreciate and embrace difference, continuously reminding anyone he could remind, whether or not they needed reminding, the importance of relishing one's own peculiarity. It all went back to Wink's short, but extremely impactful relationship with Seymour S. Seymour. Mr. Seymour, who Wink always called with the formality of Mr. except on the last day of Mr. Seymour's life when he called him Sy, taught him, much to the delight of Mel and Sylvie, how becoming an adult was being comfortable with their own specialness and saw the uniqueness of others as an asset.

This particular morning was a bit misty, as the early fog had not fully retreated. The air was perfumed with the smell of the purple lilacs in full bloom outside their bedroom window. At precisely 6:00 a.m., as he did every morning, Rex plopped her front paws on Sylvie's side of the bed and gave a short, muffled bark. This was a behavior Rex learned from the prior Rex, who had learned it from the preceding Rex, and so on. There was no sixth Rex in the household as yet. The current Rex was approaching ten years of age, which is when Mel and Sylvie always went on the hunt for the next Rex, who would then be taught all the necessary behaviors by the more mature Rex. Needless to say, Mel and Sylvie never had a need for an alarm clock. Sylvie opened her eyes and looked into a white lower muzzle and a dog's mouth open with a welcoming pant and tongue hanging loosely to one side.

"Okay, my sweet Rex. We're getting up. Meet me at the back door," whispered Sylvie. Rex turned and immediately trotted to the back kitchen door where she waited for Sylvie to let her out for her morning doggy business.

Even though Mel and Sylvie were both octogenarians, they never saw the end of having a Rex in their lives. Fortunately, they had raised Wink to be a dog lover and knew that he and their daughter-in-law Pinky would eventually inherit whatever Rex remained after they were gone. They believed passing on a Rex assured some level of immortality. Little did they know that they both had about twenty years left and wouldn't be going anywhere till they were in their 100's. There might even be another two Rexes in their future. Walking, good nutrition, and apparently good genes boded well for them. Sylvie told others, who asked what kept them young, that it was the love of dogs, morning stretches and walks, sensible diet, a large glass of good red wine every evening, and a husband with strong hands. The strong hands reference mystified those who asked. Sylvie never elaborated; she simply smiled.

This morning's walk was intended to be a prelude to a bigger celebration. It was the 50th anniversary of Mr. Seymour's death, and Wink would be marking the occasion at the former Visions of Eden retirement home, where Mr. Seymour lived during the five years Wink knew him as a grandfatherly figure. Mel and Sylvie looked forward to the evening's red beret celebration and decided to don their jaunty berets on their morning walk as an early tribute to Mr. Seymour's penchant for his singular trademark article of clothing.

Mel and Sylvie still lived in their first home, a modest house in a neighborhood of modest homes. It was always freshly painted, the yard festooned with perennial shrubs and seasonal flowers. The lawn having been removed for a more bee-friendly and water-conserving front yard. Other than two new roofs and a remodeled kitchen, they still found that after over fifty years in the same abode it was all they ever wanted. The small backyard similarly landscaped as the front with the only indulgence a hot tub. Mel and Sylvie enjoyed a dip almost every evening, especially the cooler ones, and always in the buff. The neighbors initially complained about their immodesty, but quickly decided they were simply an odd but lovable couple. And why not skinny-dip in one's own backyard. The few new neighbors who moved in over the years were forewarned by the seller's realtor but didn't complain. And they stopped looking after a few peeks. Socially ancient, although fit bodies, were not a peeping Tom's cup of tea.

Mel, a stone mason by trade, had built a low wall enclosing the front yard. His usual work involved constructing brick or concrete block walls or facades for large, contracted jobs. The wall he built for his own residence had been inspired by a vacation to Bear City where he learned of the walls built by a local legend. Wilbur's walls had become historical sites that drew visitors who sought ideas for their own projects. Mel had heard about Wilbur but never had the pleasure of meeting him. After visiting several of Wilbur's artistic constructions, Mel decided to build one of his own. He took great pride in completing a low, serpentine wall of river rock with Wink's assistance. They spent the better of a summer on weekends building what Sylvie called the Great Wall of Mills. It enclosed a planting bed filled with rotating seasonal color, tulips, petunias. irises, and whatever was on sale at the local Planet Plant Garden Shop. There was also a colorful display of red and white roses, which Mrs. Gillespie, their grandson's former kindergarten teacher, had gifted them. Over the years Mrs. Gillespie had become a special friend due to her ongoing support to their grandson Seth after his younger sister Rose's death and her famously reported anti-firearms protest with Mr. Seymour's grandson Stanley.

As it turns out, Mrs. Gillespie and Stanley had also become neighbors. Mr. Gillespie had died after a brief illness and bequeathed his entire estate to his best friend and former wife Mrs. Gillespie. Stanley had also lost his wife after her long, difficult bout with cancer. He subsequently purchased Mr. Gillespie's home from Mrs. Gillespie. Their friendship, which began with a common purpose through a demonstration against gun violence, was now a friendship separated only by a picket fence and an explosion of red and white roses.

Mel and Sylvie closed their front door without locking it. Despite the changes in their city, they continued to believe their neighborhood was a safe refuge without the need to keep the front door bolted unless they were going to be gone for an extended time. Mel and Sylvie rarely traveled. Their idea of a vacation was spending an evening at a close friend's home for a barbeque, birthday or anniversary celebration, or taking care of their grandkids Seth and Boyd. Since their grandkids weren't kids anymore, they hoped for the possibility of great-grandchildren. That seemed an impossibility since Seth and his wife Jenny declared early in their marriage that they would not be bringing children into a world that had become too dysfunctional for a positive future. Additionally, their own marital dysfunction and divorce put an end to any remote possibility of them bearing great-grandchildren. Shortly after the divorce, Seth declared himself a confirmed bachelor. He told his family that there were two binary choices in life: "happily single or miserably married, and I'll choose happy." And Boyd continued to be on an impossible quest for the perfect woman, preferably, as he put it, an exotic sabra. Mel and Sylvie accepted the notion that the Mills family legacy might end with their grandsons. The loss of their granddaughter Rose compounded their dismay. They never accepted the loss, although they had found a way to be forgiving without knowing whom to forgive. They remembered a time when Mr. Seymour talked about life as a complicated stew, "Even when you add the same ingredients, the taste is never the same. There are no repeats in life, just the next day till there aren't any."

They walked with Rex dutifully trailing behind. They never leashed Rex after initially training him, along with prior Rex's assistance. He never showed any signs of prey drive. Squirrels, birds, other dogs, small children, and others who might call out to him, either known acquaintances or strangers, could not dissuade him from his duty as a faithful, obedient walking companion. There were a few uptight citizens who infrequently chastised Mel and Sylvie for not obeying the city leash laws. However, even the local police knew Rex, offered treats when they were given permission, and accepted Mel, Sylvie, and Rex as a special exception to any and all pet ordinances. Today they walked by the former Visions of Eden retirement home, now renamed Visions Luxury Condominiums. The retirement home had long ago been closed and shuttered, as it was no longer profitable to provide long-term housing and eventual care to an aging population. There was no longer profit in serving retirees. It sat vacant and in decline for several years before investors purchased and converted the property to upscale housing. The front façade had been given a makeover with a light marble veneer, black window trim, and lighting which illuminated newly planted trees. To locals, it looked like a Disneyland residence; to out of town buyers it looked like a status symbol.

The homeowner's association management was happy to rent out their common space for a private party to celebrate the anniversary of Mr. Seymour's passing, although a few condo owners raised polite objections asking why the room would be rented out to someone not connected to a property owner. When the history was explained by management, the objections faded.

As they walked, the fog thickened. Mel remarked that a hot day further inland was pulling in a thicker blanket of fog. Sylvie felt that it was a foreshadowing for something other than a celebration, but she couldn't put her finger on what the thought meant. One of the benefits of living in a coastal environment was natural air conditioning and no need to have an extensive collection of winter ware. Strolling by Visions, they noticed three gardeners tending to the extensive drought-resistant planting beds filled with native plants, grasses, and trees. Gheorghe, the maintenance supervisor who Mel and Sylvie came to know from their walk, looked up from his weeding. He was a short, compact man who wore a broad-brimmed straw hat and dangled an unlit cheroot from his broad lips. He never lit the cheroot because his dental hygienist warned him about mouth cancer and tooth loss from smoking. The loss of teeth worried Gheorghe more than anything. He could not imagine a toothless smile, and he was always smiling. He greeted Mel and Sylvie with his trademark gleaming smile and heavy Moldavian accent. He was proud to have immigrated from a country he no longer found safe and with a dubious future. He knew about the Mr. Seymour celebration because he would be in charge of setting up the room. He had a lengthy conversation with Wink when the arrangements for the party were made and listened to several stories Wink told about his short, yet significant, time with Mr. Seymour

He noticed the red berets and said, "You are a bit early for the Seymour party. We won't fix up the room till this afternoon."

"Oh, no, we're just out for our morning walk," said Sylvie. "We will be wearing the red berets all day. They're fun."

"Oh, your son Wink told me so much about Mr. Seymour and his love of red berets and red Vans shoes. Isn't America a great country where you can wear whatever you want?"

Mel tipped his beret in Gheorghe's direction, "Let's hope it stays that way."

Sylvie felt that Mr. Seymour's grandfatherly influence on Wink, although for only five years, had perhaps been the greatest positive effect on Wink's life. He made him comfortable with his exceptionalism. It was a rare time when Wink didn't quote Mr. Seymour, even if those quotes may have been made up in the moment.

"Mr. Seymour told me that wiggling my finger when shaking left hands was a sign of acceptance and gratitude," said Wink to his wife Pinky.

"Did he really?"

"If he didn't, he would have," replied Wink.

Mel and Sylvie walked past the city park and its encampment of homeless persons, passed by the medical building where Wink and Mr. Seymour first met when Mel was having a worrisome growth removed by his dermatologist Dr. Chan. Ironically, Dr. Chan died from a melanoma but the medical building remained. They looped back towards their house looking forward to their regular breakfast of oatmeal, orange juice, fresh fruit, and coffee for Sylvie, black tea for Mel. Rex knew when they were headed home and her tail seemed to rise a bit higher and her steps became a little jauntier. Her first meal of the day was waiting, too.

The front door was ajar and Sylvie turned to Mel, wide-eyed with alarm, and suggested they call the police before entering. Wink suggested they hadn't fully shut the door and a gust had probably pushed it open.

"I'll peek inside and make sure all is okay."

"No, Mel, this is not right. Let's call the police."

"I'll just take a quick look-see."

Mel never entered. Approaching the door he noticed an unaddressed envelope on the door sill, which he picked up, opened and read the enclosed note. He turned looking like someone who had just been informed of an untimely death. A tear appeared on his cheek, his left hand holding the empty envelope trembled, and he held out the note to Sylvie before pulling it back.

"I can't believe this."

"What is it Mel? What's wrong."

"I'll read it to you." They stood facing each other with blank looks for a few seconds before Mel said they needed to go inside and sit down first.

"No, Mel, it's not safe."

"Whoever left this note didn't go inside. I'm sure of it."

They sat together on the sofa. Rex sensed something not right and curled up on her dog bed. Like all of their dogs, she had an innate sense of joy and sorrow. At this moment, she felt more confused.

Mel read the unsigned note with the solemnity of a funeral director. It was printed using a computer on plain paper, which made it unlikely to be traceable back to the sender. It read 'I'm so sorry. I never intended to harm anyone, yet I killed your granddaughter Rose. I want you and your family to know I suffer. I suffer alone.'

It had been over twenty-five years since two-year old Rose was anonymously struck down while playing on her front lawn while her mother Pinky sat on the front porch drinking her morning coffee. And now, an anonymous note, like that anonymous bullet, only this time striking into the hearts of Mel and Sylvie on the same day they were going to gather and celebrate the memory of Mr. Seymour.

Reunion

8:00 a.m.

It appeared that Mrs. Gillespie was becoming progressively smaller, if that was even possible. She was a tiny infant, the shortest student through childhood and adolescence, and diminutive as an adult. She would have shopped at the children's section of the one and only department store in town, but the fashions were not fashionable for a woman in her 80's. She made most of her own clothes as a kindergarten teacher for over forty years, but retirement meant the end of plain, conservative, and usually dark, modest dresses. Now, it was denim from the boy's section and small T-shirts wherever she could find them. She once stood just under five feet. The last time she was measured she was several inches below that defining barrier between short and little person. What hadn't changed much was her older person's appearance. Her prematurely gray, curly hair had become more of an electric coil white. Her wrinkled skin more deeply wrinkled. Her teacher's high-pitched, attention-getting voice had morphed to a lower, sandpaper textured tone. What hadn't changed was her energy and commitment to a cause.

She spent most of her days working in her front and back yards tending to red and white roses, which needed constant pruning and mitigation of aphids by spraying the bushes with a mixture of water and dish soap. She wore a large sombrero, which she purchased after arriving home from Mexico. It was the only time she had ever traveled outside the United States. In fact, the only time she traveled any significant distance from home. The trip was a gift presented to her upon her retirement, which required her to apply for a passport, which she found an inconvenient necessity. She fondly remembered when more than twenty former students wearing her trademark smocks purchased at the annual fundraiser auction presented her with the gift of travel. Those smocks permanently stained by five-year old fingerpainters were sentimental favorites at the auction and she couldn't help but laugh when they handed her a box containing the travel documents and a smock from the "**SHOOT ME FIRST**" protest that Stanley had begun after Rose's murder. She felt travelling was more trouble than it was worth, but she was deeply appreciative of the gesture and grateful for the large hats sold at the airport terminal upon her return. She figured one practical memento, even though bought at an American airport after her trip, was worthwhile. It was several months later when she noticed the Made in Vietnam paper tag. Fortunately, she was a strong believer in a global economy.

It was 8:00 a.m. and she was trimming a Mr. Lincoln rose bush when she heard her phone ringing inside her house. She only had a landline believing that cell phones were for the younger generation or old folks who might be in need of emergency medical attention. Her neighbor and good friend Stanley frequently urged her to switch to a cell phone "just in case."

"They make these gadgets as a convenience to us older folks," said Stanley.

She told him that if he ever found her passed out in her garden or not responding to a knock on her door to feel free to make the necessary call using his "convenient" phone. Mrs. Gillespie was clear to anyone who asked that growing old was more in the mind than the body. And she wasn't about to allow technology to tell her otherwise.

"No, Stanley," she would reply. "They make these things to make money and distract us from what's really important in life, hard work and the slow processes of imagination and creativity."

"That sounds a lot like something my grandpa Seymour might have said."

"I suppose that's true."

By the time she got to the phone, it had stopped ringing. She didn't have voicemail and thought if the call was important, the caller would call back. She was hanging up her turquoise Princess phone, purchased in the early '90's and still reliable, when Stanley opened the front door with the look of concern, unblinking eyes and bent forward like a pizza delivery person who suddenly realized the wrong pie was in the box.

"What is it Stanley? You look alarmed."

"Sylvie just called and said there was an emergency and you need to call her right away."

"An emergency? That must have been her calling. Did she say what it was all about?"

"Just that you need to call her right away. Something to do with

Rose."

Mrs. Gillespie wasn't much for phone conversations when it came to an emergency. Mr. Gillespie passed on shortly after being diagnosed with severe congestive heart failure. The final heart attack came while he was walking to the market to purchase his favorite mint chocolate chip ice cream. Even though his doctors insisted he change to a more heart-friendly diet, he didn't see the point.

"What do I get? Another few months of wretched foods? I'll drop dead with the pleasure of knowing I've lived a tasty life."

He ended up face planting on the sidewalk with a pint of ice cream melting by his side. The emergency contact number he wore on a copper, chain link bracelet listed Mrs. Gillespie's phone number.

"I'll be right down," she said when the hospital called. "I don't want details now. I'll be there in person."

She immediately drove her 1960 Caribbean green and snowberry white Nash Metropolitan, which Mr. Gillespie had purchased at an auction for her in 1982, to the hospital. It was fully restored and had been kept immaculate ever since, rarely recording over 2,000 miles a year. Mrs. Gillespie washed it weekly and gave it a hand waxing every Valentine's Day in memory of her former husband and best friend. The attending physician informed her that Mr. Gillespie's death came suddenly without much the paramedics could do.

"It wasn't unexpected," said Mrs. Gillespie, dry eyed with a sense of finality. "Mr. Gillespie and I knew the day was near."

The tears she shed came much later, when she was informed that she had inherited Mr. Gillespie's complete estate. He had no living relatives and had left everything in perfect order. There were a few papers to sign, a house to be emptied of its contents with most going to charity, and a sale of the house to recently widowed Stanley, who had been one of Mr. Gillespie's colleagues at the community college. After Stanley's wife had passed, he wished for a fresh start without all the memories their home contained after a long marriage. One of his son's purchased his home and Stanley bought Mr. Gillespie's. Living next door to his good friend helped with the grieving process.

Mrs. Gillespie did not call Sylvie back. She drove to her house in her Nash that was recently converted from gas to electric with all the modern dials, gauges, and computer components found in expensive factory-built electric vehicles. Mrs. Gillespie liked the idea of driving around in a car that looked like a scoop of pistachio ice cream over vanilla with all the luxury of environmental friendliness.

When asked why she spent so much money on automobile

technology while eschewing cell phones and other personal modern devices, she said, "Technology for the common good benefits the world. Cell phones, Moby Dick watches, and fancy-schmancy computers are ego-driven wastes of time that create more inconvenience than convenience. Besides, I may be one not leaving the planet the way I found it, but at least I'll try to make a difference."

The door was still ajar when Mrs. Gillespie arrived. She gave a three-beat knock before pushing it completely open and saw Mel and Sylvie seated on their sofa. The note from Rose's killer lay on the coffee table alongside Sylvie's cell phone. Rex curled at Sylvie's side.

"You didn't call back," said Sylvie with the wispiness of a voice trying to be found.

"Emergencies necessitate presence among friends." Mrs. Gillespie sat in the wingback chair across from Mel and Sylvie. She managed to lean forward even though her feet did not touch the floor. She knew from experience that body language and patience invited explanation and confession. She waited expecting neither.

Few people knew Mrs. Gillespie's first name. Her students called her Mrs. G. She always introduced herself as Mrs. Gillespie to her students' parents. Younger colleagues called her Mrs. Gillespie. Veteran teachers, administrators, and friends were the only ones to use her first name.

"Bella," muttered Sylvie, "Something disturbing has happened and we need your friendship to help us figure out what to do."

Mel told Mrs. Gillespie how he and Sylvie returned home and found the unsigned note just inside their front door. He read the note once and Mrs. Gillespie asked him to read it a second time before responding.

"He must have known your morning routine. I'll bet he watched you leave before opening the door and dropping the note inside. He knew you didn't lock the door."

Sylvie asked, "Why are you so sure it's from a man?"

"Because women don't go around anonymously shooting others."

"Why this day, of all days to leave a note with such a heart wrenching message? Wink has been planning Mr. Seymour's tribute for months. The coincidence is chilling," said Mel.

"This is no coincidence," responded Mrs. Gillespie. "Coincidences are only for those who believe in conspiracy theories and other nonsense. No, this was planned. It is not a random act. I wouldn't be surprised if the so-called unknown killer isn't that unknown. No, I think this creep probably chose today because he knows about tonight's event. The murder may have been unintended but this note was not."

Mel and Sylvie sat holding hands, staring at the note on the coffee table. Mrs. Gillespie kept her blue eyes focused on her friends.

Mel asked, "Bella, what do you think we should do. I'm not sure that today, of all days, is the best time to tell Wink."

"This is evidence. Even though the case went cold a long time ago, we need to call the police. I wonder if the detective who was originally investigating is even still working."

"You're right," said Sylvie. "I'll call. Maybe we shouldn't touch the note anymore."

An officer arrived shortly after Sylvie reported the incident. Although it had been many years since Rose's murder, it was a tragedy that was always fresh in the community's memory. While the original detective had retired, other veteran officers ensured that rookies were well-informed of the case. Every tip was followed up, whether or not the informer seemed legitimate or not. The officer who responded to Sylvie's call secured the note in an evidence bag, listened intently as Mel and Sylvie described how they found the note, and called for a tech to come out and check for the possibility of fingerprints left on the door. He asked Mel, Sylvie, and Mrs. Gillespie to remain inside and not touch any surface near where the note was found until after the tech had finished. He suggested they use a back door should they need to leave. Fortunately, the tech arrived as the officer was completing his notes.

It was less than an hour before Mel, Sylvie and Mrs. Gillespie were left alone. Mel and Sylvie were worn out by the morning's drama. They sat slump shouldered and leaning against each other for support. Rex sensed a change in the emotional chemistry of the moment and curled up closer beside Sylvie. Mrs. Gillespie, on the other hand, stood and paced behind her chair with the energy of a former kindergarten teacher.

"Bella, what are you thinking. I can tell you have a plan," said Sylvie.

Mrs. Gillespie stopped, stood as tall as an under five-foot woman possibly could, and with a voice reserved for the closest of friends said, "We need to call Stanley. We need another brain in this mix to figure out how to not keep this a secret from Wink and Pinky and also preserve this evening's celebration."

"I'm not sure that's a good idea," said Mel. "I'm sure the police will be paying a visit to Wink and Pinky right away. We should call them first. Let's not keep this a secret. It doesn't do anyone any good. Also, I'm wondering if we weren't the only ones to get a note."

"I hadn't thought of that. Let's give them a call and see if they're home and ask if we can drop by. I don't think this is news to share over the phone."

Mel made the phone call but no one answered. He surmised that they might be running errands for the evening's event. Mrs. Gillespie suggested they go over to their house and wait for them there.

"Let's stop by Stanley's and ask him to come along."

Sensing that changes were coming, probably involving a car ride, Rex jumped off the couch and waited by the front door. He carefully sniffed at those areas the police tech had checked for fingerprints and determined there was nothing else he could add to the investigation. Mel and Sylvie understood Rex's special powers, but Mrs. Gillespie suggested that Rex should stay home because they were about to enter into a sensitive and most likely emotional situation.

"This is not really a time for a standard poodle."

Rex reacted to Mrs. Gillespie's dismissive statement with a quick bark. And Mel quipped, "There's really nothing standard about Rex. He goes everywhere with us." Rex gave another sharp bark and waited for a leash to be clipped to his collar.

Mrs. Gillespie offered to drive. Sylvie had managed to wedge herself behind the front passenger seat and sit sideways in the tight quarters. Rex leapt in without any hesitation. Mel sat in front and was jolted back into his seat as a result of the electric motor's G-force acceleration. Sylvie, who was holding her cell phone, had it jerked loose and it fell to the floor.

"Sorry about that," said Mrs. Gillespie. "It takes a while to get used to an electric motor. This car is like a hot rod."

Mrs. Gillespie pulled into her driveway. Stanley was tending to his roses in his front yard and gave a wave as Mrs. Gillespie exited her car and began walking over to him. Sylvie twisted to pick up her cell phone and noticed that a text message had come through. It was from Wink and asked her to call right away. 'I received a troubling note this morning.'

Reunion

10:00 a.m.

Her death came without any surprise. It was her ophthalmologist who first suggested she see a specialist after she complained of blurred vision that seemed to come out of nowhere. By the time she saw a neurologist, she was having difficulty walking a straight line and forming coherent thoughts. Glioblastoma would define the last months of her life, barely giving her time to grieve and make her last wishes clear to her husband Stanley. The one quality that did not change was her directness and dry sense of humor.

"If this is the way I make my exit, then make sure I do it with the taste of rocky road ice cream. And preferably while licking it off your lips," she told Stanley with a diminishing, but still alluring husky voice.

She made sure their marriage always had a certain sauciness to it. She tempted him with lacy lingerie, oysters, tango lessons, and even a bit of phone sex when he was away at academic conferences. Before becoming terminally ill, she took pride in keeping herself fit and as toned as a mother of two sons could be. In terms of looks, wit, and smarts, Stanley knew he had married up. When it came to romance, though, Stanley lacked imagination. He had agreed that a monthly date night was a good idea. However, he had no idea how to make it special. Dinner out, a play or movie, and a hotel for a couple of hours while a babysitter took care of the boys was all her idea. Stanley was happy to go along with whatever she wanted.

The last days of her life were spent in a morphine-induced coma, at home, and with the care of a hospice nurse. She was surrounded by Stanley and her two sons, breathing evenly before taking several jerked breaths and going still. The nurse listened for a heartbeat before confirming she had passed. Stanley caressed her forehead, leaned over, and gave her one last kiss before turning to his sons in a tearful embrace.

During the time when decisions were being made, she insisted on a cremation and no elaborate funeral. If there was to be any kind of celebration of her life, she wanted Stanley to take close family and friends out to dinner with the promise of no sad storytelling.

"And spread my ashes in the backyard. I spent a lot of time there trying to get something pretty to grow and was never that successful. Maybe I'll do a better job in my afterlife. Also, make sure your life goes on. Find another woman. Don't be alone. Sell the house. I think one of the boys might want to buy it. Sell it cheap. You don't need the money. Get a fresh start. Don't be rooted in the past. We all end up in the same place eventually. We've loved well. Make sure to serve rocky road for dessert at the dinner you host. Don't worry if someone has a nut allergy. They can take care of themselves."

She had a way of using her words surgically, making sure meanings were clear, and giving direction to her often-directionless husband. She adored Stanley's absent-minded professor's persona and accepted his often unpredictable and impetuous nature. She found the time he began a one-person protest out of a sense of personal duty endearing and not totally outside the realm of his often-unexplainable behaviors. Others thought of Stanley as a bit of a bore and one dimensional. She knew his complexity was hidden behind a quiet shyness and a huge heart.

As instructed, Stanley did sell their house to their oldest son, who thrived in nostalgia. He was the family historian and keeper of all discarded photos, old, recorded albums, and any number of tchotchkes found packed away in the garage or attic. And Stanley ended up purchasing the house left by Mr. Gillespie to Mrs. Gillespie. Stanley and Mrs. Gillespie had become close friends after the "**SHOOT ME FIRST**" demonstrations, and he now had the honor of calling her Bella. Both had been widowed and both found comfort in their similar ages, political persuasions, and secular beliefs. Stanley's wife had urged him to find another lover after her passing but Mrs. Gillespie was not what either she or Stanley had in mind. Stanley was tall and Mrs. Gillespie far from approaching his stature. Stanley soft-spoken, while Mrs. Gillespie was clear-voiced and bordered on loud. Stanley had shared his wife's final wishes and Mrs. Gillespie vowed to help him achieve those wishes.

"There are lots of women out there, Stanley. I'd suggest you wait a year or so before pursuing." She always called him Stanley, not unlike his wife, whenever she was being serious. All other times, it was just Stan.

"I'm not sure I'm up for any sort of pursuit, Bella."

"You will be. I just don't know if you'll be fast enough. There's a high turnover at our age. You've got to act fast when opportunity knocks."

Opportunities had not yet come, but the friendship between Stanley and Mrs. Gillespie had deepened. They turned to each other whenever faced with a difficult circumstance. Lots of iced tea, lemonade, and multiple bottles of fine wine had been shared on their respective porches while mulling over challenging issues.

On the day Mrs. Gillespie pulled into her driveway after hurrying off to find out what was such an emergency at Mel and Sylvie's, he was clipping roses that grew along their shared fence. He had a collection of red, white, yellow, and lavender flowers gathered in a large, hoop-handled wicker basket and waved at Mrs. Gillespie as she exited her electrified Nash Metropolitan. She was just about to acknowledge Stanley but suddenly turned on her heels and called back to Sylvie who had just extricated herself from the small vehicle's backseat.

"What did you just say, Sylvie?"

"Wink just texted that he and Pinky have received a note."

Mrs. Gillespie turned back toward Stanley and shouted, "Stan, we've got a problem and we need your help."

Stanley called back, dropping his garden shears into the basket, "What's going on, Bella?"

Mel, who was now standing next to Sylvie and Rex, called over to Stanley before Mrs. Gillespie could answer, "Rose's killer has sent notes to us and apparently now to Wink and Pinky. We need to get over to their house right away."

Mrs. Gillespie walked over to her side of the fence, faced Stanley, and quickly filled him in. "It's crazy, Stan. And now, apparently Wink and Pinky have a second note.

"Bella, have the police been notified?" asked Stanley.

"Yes, they've already come and gone from Mel and Sylvie's."

Stanley instructed everyone to gather on his porch before doing anything else. He had an innate skill to bring calm and reason to a crisis. When others around him seemed out of sorts, he was able to center himself and get others to follow. He told them he was going to call Wink and Pinky before they proceeded to do anything else. Mrs. Gillespie, shaking her head with signs of frustration, realized Stanley was correct. She, Mel and Sylvie, with Rex sitting up in anticipation of being needed for something, were sitting on the white wicker chairs Stanley had added to the porch shortly after purchasing the house. He was a big believer in what he referred to as 'porching.' He would extol on the virtues of sitting out front during prime walk-by times, usually just before and after dinnertime, when neighbors strolled by and waved or said a few pleasantries about the weather, houses for sale in the neighborhood, or the lack of decent street repair. He always kept a pitcher of some beverage and extra glasses for those who invariably took up a chair and stayed for a longer conversation.

"Hey, Siri, call Wink and Pinky," he instructed the latest model iPhone. Belonging to an age of what Stanley called "the ancients" didn't mean having antiquated methods of communication. He put his phone on speaker and Wink answered on the third ring.

Stanley informed Wink of who could hear their conversation, reviewed what he already knew about the note left at Wink's parent's house, and asked Wink to tell them about the note he and Pinky had received. Stanley spoke with the authority learned after a long career as a college professor. He kept his sentences short and factual, without any interpretation or speculation. Mel and Sylvie remained subdued and petted Rex who was sitting between them like a Swiss guard. Mrs. Gillespie, leaning forward and prepared to chime in, kept herself remarkably subdued. She had a high level of trust in Stanley and knew when to distance herself from overstating the situation.

Wink thanked Stanley for filling him in. Stanley could hear Pinky in the background echoing her thanks. Wink then asked Pinky to describe how she found the note after they had returned from purchasing some last-minute items for that night's 50-year Red Beret Celebration. She read the note.

Pinky's mother-in-law Sylvie blurted, "It's exactly the same as the note we found." Mel placed his hand on Sylvie's shoulder while Rex looked up with open, empathetic eyes. She added that the first thing they did after reading the note was call the police. "We are waiting for them to arrive."

Stanley suggested that they should wait till after the police had done their job before heading over to Wink and Pinky's. "It's probably better if we don't get in their way. Your mom and dad and Bella have already spoken to them."

Wink asked, "Do you think this has anything to do with tonight's party?"

That's when Mrs. Gillespie spoke up. "No doubt it does. This is someone's thoughtless ruse. It's not a coincidence."

"We all want to know who this person is. I have feeling that he or she," but before Stanley could finish his sentence Mrs. Gillespie interjected, "A he for sure! Women don't play this kind of cruel game."

And then Stanley finished, "I have a feeling that he," said with emphasis, "has covered his identity by not leaving any evidence tied to the note or fingerprints left at either house. Maybe the police will find a video from a surveillance camera."

"We'll be sure to ask about that when the police come," said Wink. "But I don't know of any of our neighbors who have that sort of technology."

"Neither do I," added Mel.

"I wouldn't be surprised if there's something out there," said Mrs. Gillespie. "There is no privacy anymore."

They all agreed to gather at Wink and Sylvie's later that afternoon and well before the party. There was a shared feeling that whoever was responsible for the notes would be at the celebration and they wanted to strategize over how to react should their hunch prove true.

The morning fog had long since pulled back to the ocean. The air felt clean and fresh, yet a sense of trepidation invisibly lingered. They remained on the porch with the scent of clipped roses arranged in the basket permeating. Mel and Sylvie had yet to have any breakfast and a loud gurgling from Mel's stomach alerted both Rex and Mrs. Gillespie to the need for food. She looked up at Stanley, who had been standing the entire time they were on the porch, and asked if he had any coffee or tea and, "perhaps a nosh or two?"

Stanley went inside, followed by Mrs. Gillespie, while Mel, Sylvie and Rex sat on the porch. They didn't wait long before Stanley and Mrs. Gillespie returned with a pitcher of orange juice, a carafe of coffee, and a tray with bagels and cream cheese.

"I always keep a dozen bagels in the freezer, but I bought these yesterday and they haven't made it there just yet. I can make tea if either of you want some. I'm afraid I don't have anything for Rex, nor do I have any decaf coffee."

"You are so kind Stan," said Sylvie. "You didn't need to do this. And Rex usually eats his one meal in late afternoon. This is a very significant time in our lives and you and Bella are the friends we need right now."

There are extraordinary times when friendship reaches an elevated state, where connections take on more significance than the everyday interactions friends have with one another. It is what gives meaning to the drone of days. For some inexplicable reason, this moment of special friendship prompted Stanley to think back to one of his teaching days when the subject of significance came up and he was inappropriately dismissive towards a student.

One of Stanley's history students asked what made a historical event significant. The student was one of the many who irritated Stanley with an endless string of questions that Stanley found off-putting. He thought there were students who fell into several categories of questioners. There were those who genuinely didn't understand and asked questions for clarity. There were others who wanted more elaboration, more examples, and a deeper understanding of whatever they were studying at the time. There were some who had not been paying attention, the daydreamers, who needed to find out what they had missed during their reverie. None of those students bothered Stanley. In fact, he had a special affection for the daydreamers, as he self-described himself as being a dreamer. He found their need for answers to be genuine. They all fell into the general category of there-is-no-stupid-question. And then there were those who asked questions in an attempt to appear smarter than the others, the pseudointellectual showoffs and time stealers. They were attention-getters who thrived in a self-conceived spotlight. They asked questions for the sake of asking questions and with no intrinsic wish to learn. So, even though Stanley believed the question about what makes something significant was a good question, it came from one of the students Stanley found to be a pest. He may have actually asked a good question, but Stanley gave a snarky response, "It's when there is an absence of insignificance. Much like most of your questions." That may have been the first and last time Stanley acted like the teacher he said he'd never be. After class, he took the astonished student aside and apologized.

He and that student then found themselves in a lengthy dialogue about the nature of significance, levels of significance, what made certain historical events more significant than others, who gets to determine what is and what isn't significant, and how the meaning of significance changes over time. Stanley came to like the student and the student left with a recovered respect for Stanley.

Stanley had once shared the story of the changed relationship with that student with Mrs. Gillespie one day when they were enjoying a glass of wine on her front porch. Mrs. Gillespie listened without interrupting, a unique occurrence for her, and when asked by Stanley for her opinion remarked, "What a bunch of philosophical malarky. Sometimes you take things much too seriously." Stanley laughed hard enough to snort wine up his nose.

Now, in this moment, friendship and significance were very much on Stanley's mind. Sylvie's expressed gratitude for their friendship is what made life meaningful to Stanley. When his wife was dying, they spoke of what the meaning of life meant to them. The discussion over the meaning of life had always been a vacuous waste of time, as far as Stanley was concerned. He referred to similar topics as studying one's own navel and a waste of precious personal time. But the time had changed with his wife's brain cancer and now it no longer seemed like a mindless exercise. After long conversations about faith, religion, existentialism, and other weighty topics, subjects they had never before even considered spending their time on, they agreed that the meaning of life was all about relationships and the cultivation of friendship. This situation with the notes was one of those times when friendship was all that mattered. This was a most significant time in their lives.

Reunion

Myron Speaks

I don't expect forgiveness. Accidental homicide is not worthy of it. The regret I feel makes no difference in the lives of others. Lives I've so deeply harmed. It was unintentional. At least I can't imagine I would have ever had any intention to kill a child. It was an accident and not really my fault. Sometimes guns kill all on their own. And this gun did slaughter an innocent life, a toddler, one only beginning her journey. Someone's daughter, sister, granddaughter. I've written apologies to Rose's parents Wink and Sylvie, brothers Seth and Boyd, and grandparents Mel and Sylvie. I wanted them to know I suffer alone, feeling like I live in a cave where the walls are getting closer with each passing day. I suffer for the terrible thing the gun did.

The only gun I ever had was the one I found. I know nothing about guns and I don't even know what to call the parts of a gun other than trigger, barrel, and grip. Everything else is like a foreign language. I was hiking on some nearby BLM land when I came upon a rifle propped up against a Madrone. It looked like some sort of military rifle from a science fiction movie. It had a long barrel with a slotted cylinder covering the end, black grip, and what I guessed was a cartridge for holding bullets hanging just in front of the trigger. It smelled oily.

It was a pleasant walk, the trail with a nice coating of fresh duff making the path springy and invigorating. A shaft of filtered sunlight illuminated the gun. I thought it was a sign for me to pick it up. I gave a few shouts to see if anyone was around but received no reply, other than my own voice bouncing from tree to tree. To this day, I still have no idea what kind of rifle it was. I picked up the gun and noticed that most of what was written or etched into the metal parts had been scratched off. I suppose it was done intentionally by someone with criminal intentions. There was an internal voice who told me to take the gun before some other person might use it for all the wrong reasons. Although, I've never truly considered what the right reason could be for owning such a weapon. I understand hunting rifles, but this didn't appear to be a rifle used for the purpose of feeding oneself. I thought it was a gun, like most pistols, whose only purpose was to harm another person.

I am not a hunter, never had the desire to kill for food. I'm a vegetarian. I grow things and have my own garden. I'm a tender of gardens and work as a gardener at the Visions Luxury Condominiums. I especially like working in its vegetable garden. Sometimes my boss encourages me to take some veggies home before they rot on the vine. There's also a small grove of fruit trees. I'm especially fond of apricots, but those trees only seem to bear fruit every other year.

I've been there ever since it was a retirement home and was kept on during the transition to high-end living. I never wanted to be a supervisor and I'm happy to follow the directions of my boss Gheorghe, even though I've worked at Visions the longest. He's an immigrant who is proud of being an American with the odd habit of keeping an unlit cigar always hanging from his lips. There are three of us in charge of yard maintenance. Juan is the other, also an immigrant from Mexico and one of the hardest workers you'd ever know. I remember when the boss before Gheorghe once told Juan and me to not work so fast because management might think two employees were all they needed to get the job done. After he left, Juan and I shook our heads and both agreed that we'd never shirk our duties. Gheorghe would never ask us to work slower; it's hard to keep up with him. There is something about an immigrant's work ethic that I really admire.

I grew up in a loving home. My parents were hardworking and raised me and my sisters to do well in school and find work that would make us happy. I was a good student but without any ambition to go to college after high school graduation. My father once told me that sometimes the best degrees were earned with calluses and grit.

I mowed lawns all through junior and senior high and thought I'd start my own yard maintenance business. When I got the job at Visions, I put that plan on hold and never thought about starting my own business again. I never married but I do date regularly. Most relationships end early because women cannot seem to get over the permanent grime imbedded into my hands and under my fingernails. I don't like wearing gardening gloves and, as hard as I scrub and scrub using Lava, I only get dry, cracked, and very unattractive hands with the scent of fertilizer and other landscape chemicals. My sisters have told me time and again that I may have good hygiene but it doesn't show. I am happy with my work. My parents would be proud and, if they were still alive, suggest I wear gloves and use a good quality cologne. They had a sense of humor. I wish I did, too.

What I did have was a strange habit or perhaps better referred to as an internal voice. I can only describe it as feeling like I'm living a stream-of-consciousness experience. I know that's a literary term because my twelfth grade English teacher taught us about how some writers write with the protagonist (another term I remember from that teacher) exposing their thoughts and inner-dialogue as a continuous stream. Well, I feel like I'm living in my own stream of thoughts with a voice inside me that keeps giving me directions or a commentary about what I'm doing while I'm doing it. I know I'm not schizophrenic because I don't hear voices. It's just that one time someone called me a schizoid and I looked it up. I don't have fantasies and I'm definitely not a loner. And I'm curious about things. That's why I look things up. Google has become a good friend, maybe my best friend. I prefer reading online, too. The smell of books disturbs me. Especially library books which reek of the smells from all its other readers.

When I got home with the rifle, I tried Googling what it was. It was so confusing, but I'm pretty sure it was probably stolen from an Army base or other military facility. It's just a feeling, but I trust my feelings. My father always said, "Trust your gut." Another thing he told me was to always be quiet because others don't want to hear anyone blabber on about themselves. That's why I don't chitchat when I'm at work. Gheorghe and Juan talk incessantly and I do my best to keep my head down, pull weeds, plant plants, spread fertilizer, mow the lawns, and do whatever is necessary to keep Visions looking good. If I talk at all, it's to the plants and trees, and sometimes even the grass where it appears to be struggling. I try to urge those brown spots to go green.

When then gun accidentally went off, I never mentioned it to anyone, not even my pet fish. It was an accident. An accident that came from my curiosity, not any vindictiveness or evil intention. The next day after reading about Rose's death in the newspaper, I returned to the BLM land with the rifle and a shovel, found a place far off the trail, and buried the rifle in a hole deep enough for a cemetery plot.

I report to work every day, reporting at 7:00 a.m. without exception. If I didn't feel well, I went to work anyway. If I needed to schedule an important appointment, I always did it after work. Even when I was tempted to take some time off to meet a friend…Yes, I do have a few friends!…to attend a special, once-in-a-lifetime event, I went to work. After the accident, I went to work on time, and didn't say anything to anybody. I may have pulled my sunhat down a bit lower, but I didn't change anything else. I worked.

Years passed and one day Wink came by Visions. Yes, I knew who he was. I knew he was Rose's father. I knew all about his family. Over the years, my stream-of-consciousness voice kept me informed. There were a few times when I thought my secret might be revealed but I didn't think it would do anyone any good. When Wink came by to arrange for a special party in memory of Seymour S. Seymour, I felt a tumbling out. Seymour was a bit of a legend at Visions from when it was his retirement home. There was a plaque designating the vegetable garden as the Seymour Garden, which I found hilarious because I had heard that he was not a vegetarian like me. There was a Mr. Seymour Scrapbook with remembrances and Seymour quotations in the community room library. Wink and Pinky must have spent many hours creating that book to honor him. It had been almost fifty years since he died and Seymour was still very much alive. Everyone referred to him as Mr. Seymour. I don't get that. When the topic comes up, I call him Seymour. And the topic only comes up when Wink comes around. And Wink seems to come around more and more, especially to check the vegetable garden and the Seymour plaque he installed there.

A rumbling began deep in my stomach and I felt a pressure in my head. It wasn't guilt because it was just an accident born of curiosity. I think you can be sorry without guilt. And I felt Wink and his family should know that there was someone out there who felt sorry and alone.

I could have explained that when I got home after finding the rifle, I began a close inspection. I managed to release the clip holding the ammunition. I figured the gun was empty and I aimed it at the horizon when I pulled the trigger. I was curious how it felt to pull a trigger. I had no idea that a bullet was still loaded. I thought I had removed all of them. The gun kicked back on my shoulder, yet there wasn't a loud bang. It was more like the sound of a heavy steel basketball falling on the riding lawn mower at work. A muted, metallic clunk, which carried but did not echo.

Tonight, is the party. I have to work overtime to help with setup and cleanup. It's not much, but Gheorghe asked me to help and I always say yes to work. I'll remain quiet. My notes said all they needed to say.

Reunion

1:00 p.m.

The first time Boyd and Seth had become as close as two brothers could be was shortly after Seth had been arrested for threatening to shoot a homeless person. The charges didn't stick because who, after all, would believe the allegations of a down-and-outer over the word of an upstanding member of the community with an impeccable record of knowing right from wrong. The police officer who made the arrest was admonished and Seth given an earnest apology by the chief of police. After his release, Seth shared his quiet shame and guilt with Boyd at an all-night diner named, by someone with an inappropriate sense of humor, Eats and Runs. The food was remarkably good but the motif best described as grunge. It was managed by a woman standing as tall and wide as a San Francisco 49er defensive lineman.

From that bonding moment of brotherly love, lunch at Eats and Runs became a weekly appointment as long as it was on one of the days Miss Eleanor was working. Boyd had given her the moniker because she had a habit of always quoting and sometimes singing Beatles' song lyrics in response to something Boyd or Seth said or emoted. The first time, when Seth looked like he was going to cry, Miss Eleanor quoted a phrase from the Beatles' "I Am the Walrus." Miss Eleanor looked remarkably like a walrus and the confluence of her look and the quoted lyrics caused Seth to snort and laugh. For Boyd, it confirmed his belief that life is fleeting, and as the Walrus might sing, 'Goo goo g'joob.' Despite spending time trying to give life meaning, Boyd's personal philosophy was to just keep moving. Just keep moving was his way of saying, "Just do it," but Nike had dibs on that trademark.

Now, they sat in a booth with well-worn green Naugahyde held together with silver duct tape enjoying sandwiches that could only be made in a classic greasy spoon restaurant. Seth was eating a BLT and Boyd a Reuben which had an excessive amount of thousand island drip. Boyd was an expert at controlling drip so that it fell directly onto his plate.

Miss Eleanor was refilling Seth's glass of iced tea just as a huge glob of mayo, missing the napkin draped on his right thigh, plopped onto his left thigh leaving his khaki trousers with an eventual grease stain. Seth backhanded the offending glop onto the dilapidated Naugahyde, shook his head in disgust and uttered a familiar expletive.

Miss Eleanor looked down at Seth, smiled like an experienced sex therapist whose client had just failed and said, "Ob-la-di, ob-la-da, life goes on, brah/…And if you want some fun/Take Ob-la-di-bla-da."

Dining at Miss Eleanor's with his brother had a way of moderating Seth's extreme seriousness. There was a time when he'd take Miss Eleanor's responses as a personal affront. Gradually his demeanor shifted and he began to accept her penchant for using Beatles' lyrics as a way of underscoring life's absurdities. Additionally, maybe Boyd's general comme ci, comme ça attitude was impacting him in deeper ways than even his wife Jenny realized.

Seth was in constant need of counsel and advice. He was becoming less judgmental with his binary worldview of rights and wrongs, blacks and whites, and dos and don'ts. However, he was not interested in sessions with a therapist. He thought therapy was an arcane process more suitable to the virtual rather than the real world. He believed it poor form to pay someone to listen without giving concrete feedback or advice. Instead, he could talk to his own brother who was perfectly capable of not only listening but also more than willing to dole out opinions, although Boyd's advice was often tainted by nuance, uncertainty, witticisms, and sarcasm. Seth didn't understand the sarcasm but did appreciate the wit.

They were talking about the state of the world and Seth's usual bemoaning that civilization was collapsing along with uncontrollable climate change, which was causing an ongoing pattern of weather mayhem.

"I can't understand why anyone would want to bring a child into this world."

Boyd responded, "Well, I'm riding my bike to work, only eating foods sourced within 100 miles of town, given up red meat except when we eat here, watching PBS, taking a liking to tofu, and will marry a Jewish girl if she agrees that the vasectomy I've already had doesn't get in the way of our future."

"You're being ridiculous. I'm being serious."

"I am being ridiculous to your overly ridiculous earnestness. You worry too much. Ease up and do what you can. Everything is temporary."

"What about the future for the generations following us?"

"Well, that is a problem."

Miss Eleanor called from behind the lunch counter, "Seth, there's a phone call for you. She said her name is Jenny."

Seth often left his cell phone at home. Boyd thought not being attached to an electronic leash was one of his brother's better qualities. Jenny wondered why he even bothered to own a cell phone. They had been married long enough to accept each other's peculiarities without judgment or the expectation for changes in behavior. Jenny didn't have the same sense of righteous indignation that Seth had for so many issues, but she adored Seth's passion. Their relationship was more intellectual than physical and that was just fine with Jenny. Neither wanted children and, when asked by friends why, Jenny would say she liked practicing the manufacturing of a family but wasn't interested in the long-term burden. Seth would blush knowing the truth: practice was infrequent and there was little chance of any long-term responsibility. He also thought Jenny's analogy of lovemaking as manufacturing was an awkward description although their friends thought the term was cute. Jenny's mother was appalled, and, from the first time Jenny introduced Seth to the family, wondered what Jenny saw in Seth.

"That's my wife," replied Seth. "I wonder why she's calling me here?"

Miss Eleanor placed the phone on the counter, Seth listened before saying he'd let Boyd know and then head home immediately. He returned to the booth and informed Boyd that Jenny had returned from the grocery store to find a strange note on the front step.

"It's addressed to 'Rose's older brother.'"

"Did Jenny open it?"

"No. She said she didn't even want to touch it, but she did bring it inside. This doesn't make any sense, especially with dad organizing the Mr. Seymour party for later today."

Seth left for home and Boyd finished his Reuben and asked Miss Eleanor for an iced tea refill. It was unusually quiet in the café and Miss Eleanor, holding a pitcher, squeezed her bulk into the booth across the table from Boyd, which considering her size was not an easy task.

Even seated, she looked down at Boyd who peered back with wonderment before she said, "You and your brother have been eating here for quite a while. My restaurant doesn't get a lot of repeat customers. Usually, it's worried relatives concerned about a sick relative or friend they've just seen at the hospital or someone wanting pie and coffee. We do serve good pie, especially our fruit pies. My husband makes the pies. He makes all the food. I run the front of the house. What's up with you and your brother, especially the nickname you've given me."

Boyd was struck by Miss Eleanor's directness. She expressed herself clearly and without any presumptuousness. She spoke with kindness and invitation. When she first sat down, he thought she might be coming on to him. It happened a lot with Boyd. But then she mentioned her husband and business partner. Boyd felt she could be more than a server; she could be a friend.

"Seth and I like your husband's food. He makes a good sandwich and the pies are excellent. I'm surprised you don't have a more regular clientele. We don't mean any disrespect about the Miss Eleanor nickname. It's just that you're always quoting the Beatles and we thought the name fit."

"Well, it's a funny coincidence because my name is Eleanor. And I think the Beatles are the greatest band ever."

"Good to know. From now on we'll drop the Miss and just call you Eleanor."

"By the way, I overheard your brother mention Mr. Seymour. Was he talking about Mr. Seymour S. Seymour?"

Boyd's eyes widened and he said, "How could you possibly know about Mr. Seymour? He's been dead fifty years."

"Oh, he's a legend here. He was one of the few regulars when the place opened a zillion years ago. This restaurant was founded by my husband's great grandfather who was one of Seymour's good friends. I've heard some classic stories about the two of them. Rumor has it that Seymour came up with the name of the restaurant as a joke after winning a bet with Eugene, my husband's great grandfather."

Eleanor topped off Boyd's glass, shimmied herself out of the booth with the motion reminiscent of a harbor seal, and walked back behind the counter to tend to a new diner. Boyd finished his lunch, stood and walked to the register to pay.

"My father Wink is throwing a party in remembrance of Mr. Seymour tonight. Would you and your husband like to come? I think we'd all enjoy hearing some stories passed down from your husband's great grandfather's days."

Boyd gave Eleanor the details and she said they'd be happy to attend but it would be a bit later after the next shift's cook and server arrived. "They're usually on time. My husband is Rufus, by the way. Oh, and he's a big guy, if you were wondering."

It felt like an invitation for sarcasm. Boyd paused and thought better of making some flip remark. Instead, he quoted a Melanie lyric,

"'Well, I've got a brand-new pair of roller skates/You've got a brand-new key.'"

"What is that supposed to mean?" asked Eleanor.

"I have no idea. I just like the song. Does everything require meaning?"

"You are certainly a different species of man," said Eleanor with a twinkle in her deeply set hazel eyes with lashes so long they seemed to touch her eyebrows. "I have a feeling Rufus will take a liking to you."

Boyd left a generous tip, pretended to doff an imaginary hat toward Eleanor, and noticed a stained apron top framed by the server opening in the wall behind the counter. The giant belonging to that apron bent over revealing a large, red-bearded face smiling back like a shark after a good meal.

"Good one!" bellowed Rufus. "We'll see you tonight."

Boyd's cell phone played Chopin's "Raindrop Prelude" as he was exiting the diner. Seth asked if he had arrived home and Boyd told him he was just leaving the diner. He was beginning to tell him about Eleanor and Rufus when Seth interrupted and insisted Boyd call him back after he got home.

"I have a feeling you'll find a note on your doorstep. It probably says the same thing as the note I received. We'll need to call mom and dad right away."

"What does it say."

"It can wait till you get home."

The envelope was addressed "Rose's twin brother." Boyd sat on the front porch rocker, a gift from one of his many jilted girlfriends. The pink chair came with a message to Boyd that said he should feel good rocking away his golden years alone and without a lover. It was one of the few times a breakup resulted in bitterness and retribution, but Boyd did enjoy the chair. He thought it might be one of the Dolly Parton rockers commonly sold by Cracker Barrel restaurants.

Before calling Seth, he read the note. Seth answered on the first ring.

"He says 'he suffers alone.' What kind of a fool does he think he is? We're the ones who suffer. This fool thinks he can take away our suffering by assuming it for himself?"

"What makes you think this is even from the killer. It could be somebody's idea of a practical joke," said Boyd. "You know better than anyone how sick the world has become. They even have television shows where pranks are pulled on unsuspecting people just to get a good laugh. It's like that old show Candid Camera, only with vindictiveness and mean-spirited humor."

"Yeah, there's a world for the general public and then there's the world we live in. Our family. Big difference. And he claims it was an accident! Well, it's not an accident when you've waited this many years to apologize. It's time to call mom and dad. Of all the days for this to happen!"

Boyd suggested that he pick up Seth and head over to their parents rather than calling with such difficult news. Seth wasn't sure of the timing. He thought they would be immersed in preparing for the evening's festivities. Boyd agreed and suggested they put off the disturbing news till the next day. Their strategizing changed when Mrs. Gillespie knocked on Seth's front door.

"Hang on, Boyd. Mrs. Gillespie just showed up and she looks serious. I'll call you right back."

"Did you and Boyd get notes, too?" asked Mrs. Gillespie.

"How did you know?"

"We're all meeting at your folk's house. Call Boyd back and tell him to head over there."

"What's going on, Mrs. Gillespie?"

"We're not sure. Have you notified the police?"

"I hadn't thought of that."

"No, problem. We'll call from your parents."

"Who else received notes?"

"Everybody."

Reunion

3:00 p.m.

They were all seated on a large, L-shaped, sectional, which dominated one end of the great room. A combination ottoman/coffee table, which Boyd once suggested could be used as a helicopter landing pad, filled the open space between the two pieces of the ecru-colored sectional. Stanley and Mrs. Gillespie sat on the shorter of the two sections; Boyd, Seth their mother Pinky, along with grandparents Mel and Sylvie on the longer leg; and Wink faced them while sitting on the ottoman. Rex was curled behind the ottoman with an eye on Wink like an umpire behind home plate. Wink and Pinky had recently remodeled their mid-century house, the one they purchased a few years after Wink earned tenure. The home where they raised their children. The home where Rose was struck down by an anonymous killer's bullet. The home they were determined to live out their own lives.

A few years ago, Pinky's mother passed on and she received a sizeable inheritance. She and Wink decided to completely renovate their home. Walls were torn down, and the living room, dining room, and kitchen converted to a great room. It was in keeping with the latest open-space trend being rendered by architects who thought walls were passe. Bathrooms upgraded. Bedrooms painted and redecorated, with the smallest turned into an office for Wink. Even the garage was redone, with sheetrock installed on the previously open-studded walls along with a custom workbench and tool racks. The front porch from where Pinky witnessed Rose's death removed and replaced by planting beds.

Boyd thought the current rage of open space was another example of the loss of privacy. As outspoken and opinionated as he could be, he never said anything to his parents about his belief that tearing down walls was an enemy to privacy. He knew better than to confront his parents, who would ignore him with smiles, knowing postures, but no eye rolls. He thought houses ought to have defined spaces where refuge could be found other than a retreat to a bedroom. If someone was cooking in the kitchen, you should be able to read a book in the living room without being watched. Over a grilled cheese sandwich at Eats and Runs, he told his brother Seth that removing walls was akin to the technology that makes communication too public and without boundaries.

"It seems that the world is becoming an endless open space. We enter modern homes without definition, without walls delineating a purpose and allowing for privacy. We walk around with ear buds and publicly communicate our thoughts and emotions regardless of who might be listening. Everybody seems to be in everybody's business. I'm telling you, Seth, all of this openness will only lead to anarchy."

"Anarchy?" asked Seth.

"Yes. Whoever thought the free flow of information and total transparency was a good thing didn't understand the necessity of a representational process. Democracy requires an organized government not a free-for-all. Our gross behaviors need to be mitigated."

"You are sounding like a philosophical son of a history professor."

"I'm not sure that's a compliment or an off-hand comment."

"Who cares? But I do know you own all that technology you are now suggesting is a threat. You're certainly not a Luddite."

"I know. I worry about my own hypocrisy."

"I'm the one always complaining that the world is crumbling. I think I'm sensing a crack in your happy-go-lucky demeanor."

"Yeah, demeanors are often a mask."

Mrs. Gillespie was the first to speak. Retired kindergarten teachers have an abundance of experience directing, herding, organizing and getting directly to the point. Mrs. Gillespie had never been shy about going first. As a short person, she used her tone of voice like an orchestra's maestro to draw attention and make her point. School principals didn't publicly mess with Mrs. Gillespie unless they wanted an insurmountable challenge. And when they attempted private negotiation, they were quickly convinced of her point of view. She was a proverbial force of nature. Yet, in this moment she was at a loss for words. She spoke with a soft, tentative voice and expressed thanks for being included along with Stanley in a difficult family situation. Pinky quickly assured Mrs. Gillespie and Stanley that they were like family and their support cherished.

Seth crossed from his length of the sectional, seated himself next to Mrs. Gillespie, and held her hand in both of his. With a soft voice matching her tone, which was uncharacteristic for a man with extreme judgmentalism, he reminded her when she held his hand so many years ago.

"I'll never lose the memory of you at my sister's funeral. Your support then and beyond has meant more than you'll ever know."

"You still remember?"

"Always."

Rex, feeling that Sylvie was about to speak, looked away from Wink, stood and stretched into a downward dog, and sat before Sylvie. Dogs have a way of knowing in advance when one of their human parents is about to act. Whether it's time for a walk, a meal, a fetch, or a mood change, it's as though they have been imbued with a fortune teller's abilities or simply sense a change in the environment through their long noses. Poodles are particularly adept at reading the room. It was no surprise to Rex when Sylvie asked, "What should we do about tonight's celebration?" The others sat searching for a response. Rex gave a single bark and returned to a curled position.

It would have been timely for Wink to answer his mother's question, but he remained quiet, scanning his wife's, son's, parent's, and friends faces who all were looking to him for answers. Yet, he sat bent forward with his elbows on his knees and his eleven fingers cradling his chin. He thought back to when he first met Pinky. She was his phlebotomist who was going to draw blood as part of his employment physical for the college where he still taught. Their playful banter, mostly her quick wit when coming up with her nickname Pinky, endeared him immediately. Wink and Pinky were inseparable then and it served to help them emotionally survive the loss of Rose and the grief that never completely diminished. Gutting and remodeling their home was more than an opportunity and a wish for change. It was also a metaphor for renewal. The bedroom that was Rose's was now Wink's office. It served a new purpose without being abandoned.

"My grandfather would have encouraged us to carry on," said Stanley breaking the lull. "It took me a long time to understand most of what Grandpa Seymour told me. When he offered advice, I felt like I needed an Enigma code breaker to get the meaning. So often he'd say something that I needed to fill in with my own words. I remember when I was twelve or thirteen, I asked what it was like for him to be my age. He replied, 'Kind of like being a spelunker whose bread crumbs had blown away.' It was years later when I figured he must have been telling me that growing up is about finding one's own way. I think this is one of those times when he'd suggest we keep finding our way, our own way without some other person trying to sabotage our journey. Tonight's celebration is part of our shared story, let's not allow whoever this creep is to mess with us."

"How can we be sure the notes were even from the killer?" interjected Boyd. "This could be some unthinkable practical joke at our expense. Someone heard about the Mr. Seymour party and decided that the timing was perfect for a sick joke. Dad, it could be a student who has a grudge with you."

Wink listened without any noticeable affect; he had the ability to hide his emotions when deep in thought. He hadn't considered the possibility his son was suggesting. Were there any of his current or former students who had issues with him? Wink had always been a popular history professor. He was seen as relevant, good humored, and fair. While almost all of his students did well on their own, he was quick to provide individual tutoring to those who struggled. He was determined that his students should succeed. Every so often, there were those students he deemed slackers. They would attempt to slide through with a minimum of effort and produce extremely sloppy work. Students rarely failed Wink's classes, and, when one did, it was usually a precursor to dropping out of college. If it was a student, how would they know about Rose and Mr. Seymour and choose this particular time to pull such a hurtful stunt.

Mrs. Gillespie, so short her feet didn't touch the floor, leaned forward and said, "You know, Boyd may have a good point. I suppose anything is possible. Maybe it would be best if we just wait for the police to figure things out and go on with tonight's celebration. Why let some fool ruin our plans?"

Seth told the group that he and Boyd had not yet filed a police report. He asked who the officer was handling the case and Mel gave him his name and cell number. Seth excused himself from the living room area and stood in the kitchen area. The group could still hear his conversation. Boyd felt a bit of subdued satisfaction over the lack of privacy options but, in this case, it didn't really matter. They were all in this together.

Most of the interaction between Seth and the police officer was less about Seth reporting on his and Boyd's notes and more about Seth listening to what the officer had to say. Seth returned to his place on the sectional. He sat slump shouldered, emphasizing his pot belly, and wished for Jenny's presence. Unfortunately, she had an emergency at work and was unable to gather with the family. Seth was used to being apart from her. They spent much of their time in individual pursuits, yet, in this moment, he wished for her support. He needed a held hand, a gentle touch on his forearm, an empathetic listener. They didn't have much of a passionate marriage but they did have one based on intimate friendship.

"The officer said they've canvassed both neighborhoods seeking witnesses or anyone with video recordings. Believe it or not, there is no video surveillance in either neighborhood. The officer thought that was amazing in this day and age."

Boyd shook his head in disbelief. His parents and grandparents appeared to live in neighborhoods that existed in the dark ages of technology. Maybe he was overestimating the scourge of electronics.

Seth went on to report that one of Mel and Sylvie's neighbors, a Mrs. Evans, did see someone wearing dark clothes, and a hoodie pulled over a baseball cap walking a small white dog, perhaps a Maltese. However, the neighbor didn't see the person's face and couldn't even tell if the walker was a man or a woman.

Sylvie spoke, "That's Addie Evans. She's always puttering in her garden when we're out for our early morning walk with Rex. She's older than Mel and me and practically blind. She gardens by nose and touch and that Maltese could very well have been an illusion."

"The officer said someone would come by shortly to pick up the notes left with me and Boyd and there would be no need for an additional interview with us. He said they'll canvass our neighborhoods, too. He said the notes were printed clearly using an untraceable generic printer and doubted they'd get any evidence, such as fingerprints."

Wink held up his six-fingered left hand indicating he had something to say. Over the years, he had learned that his difference carried a useful level of authority. When teaching, his students knew when his left hand went up it was time to pay attention. Invariably, someone would say, "It's the six," and the class would become quiet in anticipation of what Wink was about to instruct. "It's the six" was a running joke encouraged by Wink. The legacy of "it's the six" carried from term to term, class to class. He never used his left hand's authority outside the classroom. For some inexplicable reason and in this singular moment, he held up his hand. Pinky was caught off guard. She had never seen Wink draw attention to himself so blatantly. She moved across to the ottoman and sat next to her husband.

In a low voice she asked, "Are you okay, Wink?"

"Yes, but now determined." Wink dropped his left hand, grasped Pinky's right hand and gave her a little wiggle with his extra digit. Pinky leaned into Wink. The finger wiggle was something Mr. Seymour insisted Wink do when shaking hands, always shaking with the left hand. Pinky perceived the wiggle as a calming sign of affection.

"Make it your signature move," said Mr. Seymour shortly after they had first met. "Embrace your difference. It's something no one can take away from you."

Mel rose from his place on the sectional and sat on the ottoman to his son's right. He placed his arm around Wink's shoulder and said, "We want to hear what you have to say. We are all here for you and Pinky."

Wink began by thanking Stanley and Mrs. Gillespie for the love and support they had given him, his parents and his sons through the years. He mentioned that it was a cliché to say, "it takes a village" and added, "it really does."

"Mr. Seymour once told me that 'when anything is possible, nothing is probable, and the truth will never be found.' Of course, I had no idea what he was talking about."

Stanley smiled broadly and chimed in, "Exactly. It takes a while to get meaning from Grandpa Seymour's words."

"For sure, Stan. I think those words have meaning for us in this situation. Someone left notes. That someone could be the real killer or some other person, as Boyd would suggest, playing a horrific hoax on our family. I'm guessing there are other possibilities we haven't thought of. So, we really can't determine the truth because it's all possible and it's also anonymous. And that reminds me of something else Mr. Seymour once said, 'Anonymity is the enemy of truth.' At the time he told me that, he was trying to make the point to always be forthright and attach your name to your deeds."

Seth felt a shiver. He had never taken responsibility for the empty threat he made to a homeless person. His brother was the only one who knew the truth. He asked himself if he needed to rid himself of the anonymity of that act. It was a question that would go unanswered.

"What we have is no identity and no answers. We've lived with that for almost thirty years. There's no reason to think it will change. We have no way of knowing the legitimacy of the notes. We can choose to allow them to control us or not. I'm choosing to be free of their manipulation. I'm choosing to go on with tonight's celebration because the truth is with Mr. Seymour and what he taught us. If the person who wrote the notes, whether the actual killer or not, chooses to reveal himself, so be it. He will not be forgiven or given any attention on my part."

Everyone considered what Wink said. Glances passed among them like jurors who had just arrived at a verdict. Stanley stood and reached out with his left hand to shake Wink's and felt the familiar wiggle.

"Before I leave to get ready for my grandfather's celebration, I'm thinking about what Wink just said and something Grandpa Seymour told me shortly before he passed. And there is no way he could have known Wink and I would end up being history teachers at the same college. I was old enough by then to understand his words. It was simple and perfect for what we are now dealing with. 'Make your own history. Don't leave it in another's hands.'"

Reunion

50 Years Since Seymour

Much of what we do is predictable, measured by time and expectation. Planning a party for a man who died fifty years ago would seem to be predictable with easy expectations and few surprises. Wink had spent several months putting together the details to honor a man who, in five short years, had a profound impact on his life. Ages seven to twelve are formative years. According to some cognitive psychologists, it's when children develop logical thinking skills on their way to more abstract and creative thought. When Wink first met Mr. Seymour, he was seven and entering the logical thinking phase, things that made orderly sense. When Mr. Seymour died, he was twelve and well into his last phase of intellectual development. He was beginning to understand their more conceptual and philosophical conversations. Mr. Seymour's metaphors didn't seem so obtuse anymore. Those five years with Mr. Seymour, Wink's adopted grandfather, would impact Wink for the rest of his life. Wink regularly recalled something Mr. Seymour said when he needed an elder's wisdom.

Wink pulled into the visitor parking lot at Vision's Luxury Condominiums and was surprised to find all of the parking spaces occupied. Rarely were there more than two or three cars in a lot with thirty spaces. Wink thought the lot would be more than adequate for the fifteen or twenty invited guests, and it was an hour before the party was set to begin. The caterer's van was there, which was a good sign, but Wink was concerned that his guests would need to park on the street.

Wearing his red beret and red Vans, he walked up what used to be a plain, concrete walkway and now laid with interlocking pavers, he remembered when Visions was a retirement complex boasting a simple utilitarian design. It was when Visions was an invitation to anyone wanting a place to live out the last days of their lives with companionship, organized activities, and homestyle food served family-style in a dining room featuring large round tables designed for active communication. There were also a few tables for those who preferred their meals alone or with another. That Visions was affordable to those living on social security, even those who could afford a more lavish lifestyle, and those in between.

Visions Luxury Condominiums began with the new walkway's suggestion that this was a place for those who could afford only the best. The building's façade was now marble. Triple-paned windows had replaced the old casement windows that cranked out. The new double-hung windows tinted so those inside could survey the outside world, while the outside world wondered what mystery was hidden behind those windows. This Visions beckoned the upper class and those who valued their privilege without understanding what that privilege meant, or if they had any responsibility to others less fortunate.

Wink approached the former dining room and now community room, which Visions Luxury Condominiums called a gathering space. The room was no longer intended for the pleasantries of a shared meal and conversation, most often characterized by reminiscence; rather, it was a place for formal events, networking, bragging, and deal-making. Allowing Wink to hold an event honoring a former resident of the old Visions was highly unusual. Current residents complained of the potential harm to their status and reputation if anyone could use their facilities. However, Wink's contributions to the gardens, especially the establishment of the Seymour Garden, carried influence. Visions management convinced residents that the event would be good public relations, and an added plus was the rental fee would go a long way toward the purchase of a new grand piano to pair with the existing Yamaha. There were several residents who wished to play duets a la Ferrante and Teicher after they had discovered the duo on YouTube.

Off to the side of the entrance, Gheorghe and Myron were seated on a bench. Gheorghe was wearing a red baseball cap and Wink wondered if that was planned or simply a coincidence. Wink waved hello to both and Gheorghe returned the gesture with a broad grin, as he pointed to his cap; Myron sat with his head down and seemingly disinterested. Wink invited them to come inside and enjoy the festivities once guests had arrived. Gheorghe said many had already come early, which confused Wink. Gheorghe thanked Wink for his offer but said he and Myron would tend to a few garden chores until it was time for them to clean up the room after the event.

"We'll be available if you need anything else. The caterer already asked for more tables," said Gheorghe.

Wink was met inside by the caterer and about thirty people milling about. He didn't recognize any of them. The caterer quickly pulled Wink aside.

"You ordered food for twenty to twenty-five. There were already more than thirty folks here when we arrived, and many of them have brought their own food, casseroles, breads, pies, cakes, cookies, veggie platters. What's going on, Wink?"

"I have no idea. Does anyone seem to be in charge?"

"There's an older, gray-haired woman whose been arranging food on the tables I'm supposed to use. She says her name is Katie. I've already asked the two helpers sitting outside to bring in more tables, but I told them to wait till you arrived. Are you sure you have the room for tonight?"

"Oh, I'm sure," replied Wink. "I'd better talk to this Katie and see what's going on."

Katie tapped Wink on the shoulder before he had a chance to seek her out.

"Do you remember me, Wink?"

"I'm sorry. I don't know who you are."

There was something familiar about the woman who reminded him of a taller Mrs. Gillespie, not with her look but with her countenance. Her eyes were as piercingly blue as Mrs. Gillespie's, her smile suggested care and understanding, and her lipstick a bright red. Yet, she presented a much younger look for a woman who must have been about the same age as Mrs. Gillespie. Her style befitting her age but suggesting youth. She fashioned her silver hair like a young woman's bob, cut straight just below her ears. She wore a cream-colored sweater and black pants like a model for AARP magazine. She held a large black tote bag filled with what looked like red articles of clothing. Pinned to her sweater was a nametag proclaiming her "Katie."

"I'll always remember you as the six-fingered boy who befriended Mr. Seymour when I was the receptionist at Dr. Chan's office." Pointing to her nametag she added, "This is the same tag I wore for almost forty years."

"That was a long time ago."

"Over fifty years. After Dr. Chan died, I remained with the practice and retired after working for five more dermatologists. Sy, Mr. Seymour insisted I call him Sy, stopped by almost every day while on his daily walk. He became friends with many patients. You weren't a patient, I think your father was, but Sy always spoke fondly of you. He thought of you as another grandson."

"How did you hear about this party? And who are all these other people?"

Katie explained how Mr. Seymour had been such an important influence on her life and so many others. She told Wink how she was a young, inexperienced receptionist before Mr. Seymour changed her life with a few simple words.

"I was a nervous and overly serious young woman. One of the first times he came into the clinic, he told me, without being instructive, how much my ugly Christmas sweater made patients feel at ease. He then said, 'There's a difference between a serious look and a welcoming smile. I'm guessing you have both.' Over the few years I knew Sy, he often made comments that helped me discover and develop my confidence and interpersonal skills. He always lingered in the waiting room and talked to many of our patients. I asked Dr. Chan if that was okay. Dr. Chan said it was like having a personal stress reducer around. 'He's better than Prozac.'"

"I'm so glad you're here. How did you find out about this and who are the others?"

"Sy's grandson Stan has been an acquaintance for years. Stan was a patient in the clinic, and his connection to Sy made it easy for us to become friends. When his wife died, which was years after my husband's death, I thought we might pursue a closer relationship but Stanley showed no interest. He told me about what you were arranging and I took the liberty of mentioning it to a few of my friends who either knew Sy or who had relatives or friends who knew him. It's amazing how much one man's influence can have even fifty years after he's gone. I guess some of those I told relayed the word along to others. I never suggested they bring food. It just happened. I hope it's okay."

"Of course. It's really an honor to have you here. The guests I invited will be arriving soon and will be wearing red hats and shoes. It was Mr. Seymour's trademark garb. I hope you won't feel out of place."

Katie pulled a red beret from her tote. "I have enough for most of these folks. I'm afraid we'll have to do with the shoes we are already wearing." She held out her left hand as an invitation for one of Wink's famous shakes. He obliged and Katie said, "Sy had a way of making everyone feel special. Now, how about if you go and introduce yourself to the others. I'll help the caterer with the setup. It's the least I can do. And be sure to give these uninvited guests a little finger wiggle."

Wink mingled, introducing himself and discovering countless connections, mostly indirect, between Mr. Seymour and people he was meeting for the first time. Everyone had a story to tell from either personal experience or one that had been passed along as family lore. Mr. Seymour was a well-known advocate for many popular and more often than not unpopular causes. Wink heard how he had helped save an uncle's home from eminent domain. An effort that won him lasting admiration from one family and bitter disdain from an entire community trying to build a road, which would reduce commute time. Mr. Seymour had created a spider's web of personal connections that had endured normal time and expectation, something that no one could possibly predict for any one individual. As Wink circulated, he shook left hands, explained the finger wiggle and his red hat and shoes.

Katie and the caterer arranged the food and drink tables. Wink noted the easy rapport she and the caterer developed. Gheorghe had come in to help with preparations. Wink thanked the three of them for the good work and invited Gheorghe, again, if he would like to stay.

"You're more than welcome to join in. After all, you and Myron do such a good job tending to Seymour's Garden."

"No, I think it's best if I remain outside with Myron."

"He's welcome, too."

"I don't think he'd be comfortable. Myron is different. I think he may be the loneliest person I've ever known."

Katie donned a red beret and distributed the others to almost all the other guests who had just learned of their significance. Wink's invited guests began to arrive, all wearing a variety of red hats and shoes.

Stanley and Mrs. Gillespie were the first to enter the room already bustling with storytelling, laughter, and the forging of new friendships. Mrs. Gillespie's beret, several sizes too small, pinned to her gray hair like a misplaced clown's nose, and underscored by overly large red Converse sneakers. Her size made it difficult to get sizes right, so for special occasions she winged it. She gave Wink a hug, told him she had to park her Metropolitan on the street, and asked who all the strangers were.

"It's a long story, but a good one. I'll fill you and the family in later."

Katie immediately stepped between Wink and Stanley, taking Stanley's hands in her own, and giving him a look that went beyond mere friendship. Stanley wore a red cowboy hat and red galoshes that rose mid-calf. He looked like a wrangler for a pig farm.

"Grandpa always said we should find our own style. I had to work at this," said Stanley like a senior citizen rediscovering his youth after a long absence. Turning to Wink, "I take it you've met Katie. She's a real force of nature."

"No doubt, Stan."

As the room filled to near capacity after Pinky, Seth, and Boyd arrived, Wink's parents finally entered. Mel and Sylvie asked Wink to step outside for a moment. Gheorghe and Myron were working nearby deadheading a variety of perennials. Gheorghe looked over with a wave and a smile while Myron kept his head down and plucking withered blooms.

Sylvie said, "The police called us just before we left. They told us they had yet to discover anything new from the notes or their neighborhood canvassing. They indicated they were not hopeful unless whoever wrote the notes takes further action. Your dad and I are so sorry this has put a damper on tonight's celebration."

"It really hasn't. You can't believe what I found when I first arrived. Dad, do you remember Katie the receptionist from Dr. Chan's office?"

Wink quickly filled in his parents about Katie, her connection to Stanley, and her vast memory of her time working at the dermatology clinic.

"Oh, my, I think I remember her as a young woman who was shy and overly serious."

"She says Mr. Seymour changed all that. You'll be impressed."

Wink's parents went inside and Wink, again, invited Gheorghe and Myron to join the festivities. Gheorghe said he might in a bit. Myron did not reply and kept snipping dead blooms.

The room was abuzz with factual and skewed stories of connections with Mr. Seymour. It really didn't matter. A person's legacy is more often than not built on a combination of fact and fiction. Oftentimes, the inventions are far more interesting than the basic truth. Wink, now sixty-two, was twelve when Mr. Seymour died. Yet, there was a woman at least ten year's younger than Wink telling Mrs. Gillespie how she lunched with Mr. Seymour every Monday.

"He loved fish sandwiches piled high with coleslaw. He said that fish was the secret to a scaled life. I don't know where he came up with those words of wisdom."

Mrs. Gillespie nodded with acceptance, the way she would have while listening to one of the many former kindergarten pupils who told the tallest of tales without any compunction, before replying, "What a wonderful story. That sounds like something your mother may have told you, dear."

There were others, who like Katie, knew Mr. Seymour when they were young and just beginning their independent lives. Simi, was a nineteen-year-old university student from Nigeria, working as a parttime maid at the Vision's retirement home when Mr. Seymour asked her about her journey. She had gone on to become a successful attorney, married with two daughters and seven grandchildren. She stood with her husband, both wearing berets gifted from Katie. Simi carried her wealth well and without pretense. She wore a simple, high-necked black dress adorned with a single strand of pearls. Her husband, distinguished by a full, gray beard and gleaming bald head, dressed in a custom-made charcoal suit with black brogues as shiny as his pate. The most telling aspect of her wealth was an emerald-cut diamond ring large enough to cause suspicion and admiration. She held her hand casually at her side, as there was no need to wave it about as a sign that she had arrived.

"Mr. Seymour spent hours tutoring me. My English was still evolving and I struggled at university. I had status in my home country and found it difficult to understand why it didn't transfer to America. Mr. Seymour, always asked me to call him Sy, but I found it difficult to be so casual with a gentleman whose age deserved respect."

"I know what you mean," said Wink.

"I thought I would go to school, earn a degree, and return home to work in my father's business. Mr. Seymour encouraged me to find my own way. He enjoyed debating issues with me. Whatever conflict was going on in the world at that time was an opportunity to argue both sides. He had a reputation as an advocate. I thought he must have been a lawyer. He said not formally. He encouraged me to use my skill as an arguer to go to law school. He helped me with applications and put me in touch with attorneys who gave me internships and wrote letters of reference for me. In many, ways, I owe him my career and, hence, my good life."

"That's a wonderful story, Simi."

"You know, my husband and I could live in this monstrosity if we chose to. I don't think Mr. Seymour would approve."

Wink laughed and replied, "You know that's the truth! I'm so happy to have met you." Before continuing their interactions with others, they exchanged contact information.

It was obvious that the party was going well, even before any of the formal speeches were made. Stanley and Wink had prepared a few words to conclude the evening. Just before they were to speak, Eleanor and Rufus arrived, followed by Gheorghe, who had decided to leave Myron with plant maintenance.

"Is Myron going to join us?" Wink asked Gheorghe.

"No. He says he's not feeling all that well and he'll remain outside until it's time to clean up."

Boyd hurried over to greet Eleanor and Rufus, introduced them to his parents and explained the history between Mr. Seymour and Rufus's grandfather. Eleanor waved at Mel, who crossed the room with Sylvie and Rex. Much to Wink's surprise, his parents knew Eleanor and Rufus. Wink learned that his parents had been going to Eats and Runs for years.

"I didn't know you ate there."

"Your dad and I have been going for years. I'm surprised we never told you that Rufus makes the best clam chowder ever. Did you know about his grandfather's connection to Mr. Seymour?"

Eleanor leaned over to give Rex a pet. "So, this is that famous poodle you are always talking about. It's too bad he's not allowed in the restaurant, silly health laws and all."

"We've had a number of Rexes and this one is a special one. Did you know our first Rex used to go for walks with Mr. Seymour? He used to say poodles were so smart and could hunt, run agility courses like the god Mercury, pull a sled at Iditarod, and take very long naps," laughed Sylvie. "Our first Rex adored Mr. Seymour."

Wink was mildly astounded by his parent's revelation, shaking his head in comic disbelief. How could they have not told him about Eats and Runs? What else might he discover before the evening was over?

From the moment Eleanor and Rufus entered, they drew everyone's attention. First, their combined size was impressive. Together they looked like oversized enforcers from a science fiction movie. Rufus stood almost seven feet tall, Eleanor not much shorter. They were both dressed in toga-like costumes, which looked like they were made from tie-dyed bedsheets... Eleanor's a mix of purples and reds, Rufus's greens and yellows. They also wore knitted, red conical hats, which Eleanor proudly declared she had made for the occasion. Doc Marten boots, spray-painted red completed their outfits. Eleanor said the boots were old and had already served their purpose.

"Besides, we didn't want to splurge on overly priced tennis shoes we'd probably only wear once," bellowed Rufus. No doubt, Rufus always bellowed because a person of his size could not have a volume control.

What was most striking, however, was the sitar Rufus carried in. Wink wondered what Ravi Shankar would think of a giant with an immense red beard playing sitar. Eleanor explained that Rufus learned to play the sitar before they were married.

"Not only does he play the sitar, but, when we traveled to Mongolia on our honeymoon, he learned to throat sing. I first fell for him when he played sitar to woo me. The sitar, the connection to the Beatles, he was too much to resist. Combining it with throat singing was the icing on the Tuva cake, so to speak."

Eleanor asked if it would be alright to share a Beatles' song in honor of Mr. Seymour. "One of the stories handed down to Rufus was that Mr. Seymour loved this particular song. It was one of the first featuring a sitar, and we think it pairs well with throat singing."

There was a small stage with a lectern and microphone, which had been set up for the evening. Eleanor and Rufus cleared the platform. Rufus sat cross-legged and cradled the sitar. He took on the appearance of a giant musical Buddha. Eleanor stood next to her husband assuming the posture of an operatic diva, hands folded at her chest and one foot firmly planted in front of the other. Rufus plucked a few strings, tuning the instrument before nodding to Eleanor that he was ready.

Rufus began playing. Wink immediately recognized the opening of "Within You Without You," a classic from the Beatles' "Sgt. Pepper's Lonely Hearts Club Band." Slow, delicate harmonies emerged from the sitar with the skill of an accomplished sitar player. Eleanor began singing, her voice a soothingly deep contralto. It was evident from her controlled breathing that she was a trained singer. Rufus began throat singing and the resonance of the sitar with his raspy, sonorous, yet melodic, voice underscored the beauty of Eleanor's lead. The Beatles' lyrics could not have been more fitting:

We were talking about the space between us all
And the people who hide themselves behind a wall of illusion
Never glimpse the truth
Then it's far too late
When they pass away

They finished, Eleanor bowed, although not too deep given her size, and Rufus respectfully lowered his head and sitar in gratitude. The room burst into applause, bravos, with many cheeks being wiped dry from the emotion of what was just heard, Mrs. Gillespie rushed to the stage throwing her arms partially around Eleanor. Others approached Rufus to shake his hand. Wink noticed everyone shaking left hands with Rufus while including a finger wiggle in the shake.

After the lectern and microphone were repositioned, Stanley approached and offered a few words of appreciation for those attending in honor of his grandfather. He finished by saying, "I was lucky enough to have Grandpa Seymour in my life into my thirties. I wish I had recorded every piece of advice or counsel he had given me. And certainly, every wise tidbit I've heard tonight. Fortunately, his words live within each of us. I will always cherish what we've shared with one another at this very special occasion."

It was Wink's turn to speak. He had written a few prepared words but decided to abandon them and speak off the cuff. As a teacher, most of his day was extemporaneous. He prepared lessons but had to deal with the reality of the classroom, student responses to those lessons, and the need to adjust in the moment. He drew from his prepared notes to thank everyone for coming, named those who had singular significance in his life: Pinky, his sons, his parents, his brother, Stanley, and Mrs. Gillespie. He made special note of Katie, who unwittingly expanded the celebration beyond expectations.

"Today has been a day of profound surprises. Fortunately, my family, close friends, and now all my new friends, have come together to remember Mr. Seymour fifty years after his passing. But he has not really passed; he lives within our collective experiences and memories. Today was the perfect day for remembering something he told me just before he died. With his encouragement, I auditioned for a school play. I didn't get a part. In fact, the drama teacher said I should consider another artistic endeavor. I was devastated. There were some disturbing things that happened earlier today to me and my family, which I won't share because in the scheme of things they won't make a difference. What makes a difference is how we live our lives. Mr. Seymour told me when I failed to get a part in the school play that 'if you open one door and no one is there, open another door.'"

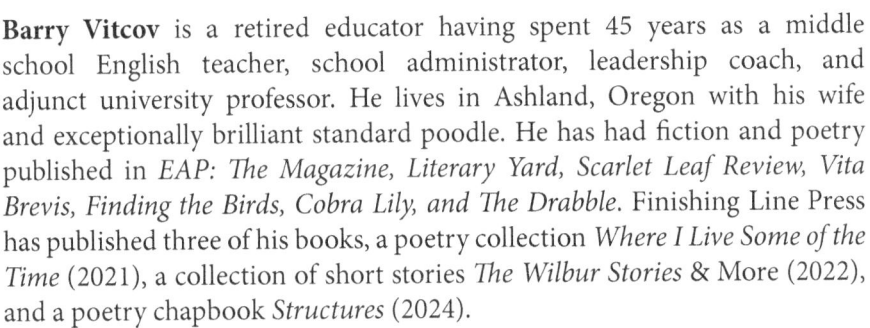

Barry Vitcov is a retired educator having spent 45 years as a middle school English teacher, school administrator, leadership coach, and adjunct university professor. He lives in Ashland, Oregon with his wife and exceptionally brilliant standard poodle. He has had fiction and poetry published in *EAP: The Magazine, Literary Yard, Scarlet Leaf Review, Vita Brevis, Finding the Birds, Cobra Lily, and The Drabble*. Finishing Line Press has published three of his books, a poetry collection *Where I Live Some of the Time* (2021), a collection of short stories *The Wilbur Stories* & More (2022), and a poetry chapbook *Structures* (2024).